Girl Gets Kidnapped

Sumit Pramanik

ALSO BY SUMIT PRAMANIK

THE GIRL BEHIND THE GLASS

FICTION

This novel is entirely a work of fiction. The names, characters and incidents portrayed in it are the work of the author's imagination. Any resemblance to actual persons, living or dead, events or localities is entirely coincidental.

About the author

Sumit is a compulsive thinker, intense listener, clumsy biker, silent laugher, inept stalker and shy hugger. His first novel, THE GIRL BEHIND THE GLASS, a suspense thriller published in 2017, was about a hotel that hides dark secrets. He successfully completed the British Council's Creative Writing Course. He is an MBA graduate from the Indian Institute of Management Indore, and he currently lives in Mumbai, India. He loves to stroll through streets, recollect last night's dream, and tell himself that it's not an addiction. Apart from writing, he adores painting and working out.

Acknowledgements

I am deeply grateful to my mother, Chhanda Pramanik, whose sharp observations of everyday incidents have taught me the importance of minute details in stories. Super-duper-mega thanks to my father, Asok Kumar Pramanik, whose political views inspire me to look at an event from all angles before judging it. I am indebted to my brother, Amit Kumar Pramanik, for his crucial feedback on my previous novel. Big cheers for my nieces, Asmi Pramanik and Urvija Pramanik, for being such brilliant sources of joy in my life. Profound appreciations are due to my close friends, G Krishnan Nair, Kari and Debapriyo Khan, who reviewed the early drafts and showed confidence in the manuscript. Thank you, @pixelwizard_ (Instagram handle), for designing an intense book cover. I applaud the efforts of all the fantastic people at Evincepub for guiding me through the process of publishing this book.

Finally, thanks most of all to you, dear reader, for always being the ray of sunlight that makes me wake up every morning and sit down to write. I hope you enjoy the story.

Contents

Chapter 1

Riju

I heard bits and pieces of the news yesterday from our porter Nelson, but he, as always, seemed to be exaggerating. He flung his skeletal arms skywards and widened his eyes dramatically. Stuttering, he spoke of ancient curses falling upon us, of dragons coming to life. Our names would be written in history because we began the end of the world, he said, only there would be no one alive to write it. I did not believe him but suspected there was something wrong.

My doubt was confirmed when I woke up to a strange silence this morning. The birds did not screech. On other days their harsh voice would startle me. I disliked them, but this quietness felt worse. And even though I was assigned a spacious tent, the soundlessness appeared to occupy the whole of it. Deafening anxiety surrounded me.

I put on my full-sleeve T-shirt and a pair of jeans. The mosquitoes in Kruger National Park were far more dangerous than its heat. A shadow appeared outside the entrance of my tent. With my fingers, I dabbed the fake laugh-lines around my lips, making sure the transparent silicone patches were in place. A female voice called out my name. I unzipped the door, and in stepped Keira Marshal, our leader.

Keira looked more like a tattoo artist than a PhD scholar. Numerous motifs were inked across her rich and dusky skin, most of them written in Sanskrit. Her face always seemed conscious of her expressions – a frown surfaced on it, disappearing the next moment. Her hair was a fountain of uncountable braids. She was the only Zimbabwean valedictorian in the Department of History at Oxford ever.

"Did you hear the news?" she said. Her voice sounded shaky.

"The news about the fire?" I asked her.

She nodded. "The semicircle on the western side gained momentum yesterday."

"How does that affect-"

"Let me finish. It also reversed its direction."

I pulled a chair and sat down. The quietness around me found my throat. Keira sat down on the table in front, her hands gripping the edge.

"You know what this means," she said.

"And which way is the eastern semicircle going?" I asked her even though I knew the answer.

"It has stayed true to its course. It is coming towards us."

"Nelson and his friends were talking about a trail between the fires that leads to the river."

"I checked," she said. "There is no river within miles. That explains the low population of animals in this area."

"But-" I started, then stopped. "I don't think we can trust them."

"You mean Nelson and his men?"

I nodded.

"I agree," she said. "They have been trying to scare us from the beginning."

The beginning. Ninety-five days ago, we had gathered near the southern gate of Kruger – a national park that spread across more than seven thousand five hundred square miles. We were a team of fifteen people from ten different countries; our governments chose us. This was not a secret mission. On the contrary, it was announced with great fanfare. The accomplishment of this project could result in the unification of nations. Of people. Of religions. Of Gods. Yes, plural – Gods.

We had been so excited about it at the start, the impossibility of the task had escaped our minds. It had been a colossal mistake.

"Although I never believed in Nelson's words before," I said, "now, don't we wish we had listened to him with more attention?"

She leaned forward. "Deven, there is no route between the fires."

"Surely-" I began.

"No," she shook her head. "We are trapped."

The finality in her tone jarred me. I pushed a water bottle kept on the table towards her. She did not touch it.

"I thought our communication lines were broken since Saturday," I said. "Then how did the news reach us?"

"There was a window of two minutes during which the receiver came alive. The head of the Geological Department was on the other side."

The canvass of my tent danced about as the wind outside picked up pace. The wind was blowing towards us, helping the fires surround us. A silent curse escaped my lips.

"Do you have any update on the military tangle?" I asked Keira.

Her face twisted in a grimace. She was upset, holding back her frustration. When our mission had been still on the drawing board, she had repeatedly asked for a special military force on standby. But it had initiated a debate. No country wanted to take up the responsibility. "This isn't a joint military drill, professor," a foreign minister had joked. "It is a peacekeeping, civilian mission." They had been busy assigning coverage rights to news channels. So finally, all the safety net we had received had been a direct communication line with the South African Reserve Police Force.

Our line with them snapped a fortnight ago, two days before the fires began.

"No word from them," Keira said. "Then there is another problem Professor Murakami pointed out."

"Let me guess. The swamps around us breathe out combustible gas."

"That comes later."

"Then?"

"The fire on the west started fifteen miles from our camp. And it has been chasing the animals within that perimeter in our direction. We crossed a pack of hyenas three days ago."

"Also, the lion family we spotted the day before."

"They are coming towards us," she said. "They are hungry and panicked."

A knot formed in my gut. "It's going to be chaotic."

She released a sigh. "You should start saying your prayers."

The irony of the situation might have deserved a smile, but it did not come to my lips. We had arrived in Johannesburg thinking that we would help people know God better; we would make them respect the Gods of others and see that theirs were no different. But instead, we ended up in a danger that left us praying to the Almighty for help.

"I find it difficult to believe in what we are pursuing," she said forlornly. "Education, after a certain point, either brings you closer to God or pushes you away from Her. In my life, the latter happened."

"Keira, I don't think we have time for this."

"We don't have time for anything," she said, "other than sitting here and embracing the end."

I placed a hand on her knee. "Then why did you agree to undertake this mission?"

"I did it for the people who have faith in Her."

My admiration for her grew. Keira was attempting the uncertain even though she did not trust it. She was doing it because she cared for those who believed in it and accepted the existence of religions.

No one denied the presence of religions. No one ever asked, "Do you believe in religions?" Although, the basis of religions were Gods. It was interesting that religions felt so solid, whereas Gods seemed, for many people, vague.

The consequence was more tangible than the cause.

"How are the others taking the news?" I asked Keira.

"The same way they take everything else. With mutual disagreements."

"That is not going to help."

"But that is what they specialize in."

It was true. All our team members were eminent people, pioneers in their fields. They were refined people who spoke in sophisticated languages, but only in public. When they talked among themselves, their polish faded away. They nurtured the feeling of invulnerability that came with success. They found happiness in arguments. Now, they could not find a solution when their lives were at stake. They must be frustrated.

But I was not like them.

And Keira, in her own way, was also unlike them. She wore funky clothes and spoke in straight words. A less knowledgeable person might say that her manners were coarse, but not me.

I hated to keep secrets from her. However, I had no other option. For instance, I could not tell her I was aware of the two minutes during which all the communication lines transmitted signals. I had received a message on my second mobile at 8:02 p.m. yesterday. My phone had taken another two minutes to decrypt the text.

It had said: *The last house still stands.*

The message had been sent from the office of the Prime Minister of India.

Chapter 2

Vikram

I sat on a chair that looked like a throne and smelled of rats. One might think that it did not matter which chair a king sat in; he remained a king. But for me, it mattered. My view from the stage made me wonder if Basirhat had ever witnessed a more significant event than this. I kept my head slightly drooped towards the right and my legs crossed at the knees. I was always aware of my posture. Right now, my stance communicated humility from a position of power.

The announcer called out my name, and I walked up to the podium. I did not touch the microphone. "Vikram," my dad used to tell me, "if you want to be great, do not ever hold the microphone. And never carry a written speech."

En route to greatness, he was butchered by four men, killed by four Muslim men.

The crowd in front of the stage now primarily consisted of Muslims. Bony men wearing skullcaps and lungis. Women who had wrapped their pallus around their foreheads like a hijab. And there were children, hundreds of them. The boys half-naked, the girls in churidars, their clothes ruined by holes and dirt.

I could not spot any angry youngsters in the audience, which did not surprise me. They must have been under the impression that this arrangement was worthless. Vikram Rathore's presence would change nothing, they must have concluded. They thought their situation could be salvaged only through violence. The idiots had no idea how many battles in history were won without sacrificing a single drop of blood and how much bloodshed had resulted in failure.

The unsettling hum that had lingered in the Lal Bahadur Maidan till a moment back came to a stop.

"Aap mere bhai ya behen nahi hain," I spoke into the microphone. "You, all of you, are my children. A brother can backstab, but a father, never. A father must inform his children when they go astray. Will you trust the words of a father?"

More than ten thousand heads nodded at the same time. Even the branches of the peepals and the gulmohars – bent with the weight of men sitting on them – swayed.

"I know exactly what you are feeling right now," I continued. "You think you are angry, but the truth is, you are frightened. You think you are desperate to take revenge, but all you want is to feel less afraid. *Dehshat main din guzarna bahut mushkil hai.* It is not for the weak-hearted.

But you want to do what is easy. When a dog bites your daughter, it is easy to kill every dog in the locality. When a man from another religion shoots your brother, you can easily hate everyone who follows that religion. The shooter's identity is not his religion, even if he says that his shootings are in the name of religion. *Humari baat samajh rahe hain aap?* If a criminal wears the mask of religion, the simplest thing you can do is attack the mask. But our duty should be to identify the person. It does not matter what mask he is wearing."

I paused. Ten massive cameras were aimed at me from different angles and distances. One of them hung from a crane. Shiva, my secretary, had informed me that Netflix was shooting a documentary based on my life.

"The shooters claim that Asif was smuggling cows across the border," I said, "but the truth is that he owned those cows. Would they have shot him if they thought he was smuggling goats or pigs or sheep? The answer is yes. Because these people fight for control over smuggling. When they were caught, they painted it as an affair of religions. *Lekin yahaan mudda dharm ki nahi, jaati ki nahi, nyay ki hai.* And justice is what the police is after. They showed extraordinary speed in arresting the three culprits. Now, this is a critical time. What you do now decides how peaceful Basirhat will become in the coming days. Last week a few men almost broke into Himanshu Pandit's house. It was utterly unwanted.

Distrust is in the air. And this is why The Vice-President of India asked Dilon Main Mohabbat to look after Basirhat. As the members of Dilon Main Mohabbat, Yadavji, Sharmilaji, and I will visit Asif's and Himanshu's houses. We will hear out their relatives, then we will visit your homes. We will meet all of you. Today evening, we will have an open Sabha with the leaders of the locality. We will understand your concerns. *Aap sabhi ko bolne ka mauka diya jayega, kyunki woh aap sab ka haq hai.* Then we will make a list of your complaints and get the authorities involved. I will personally make sure that each one of your issues is addressed within two months."

I took a gulp of water from the glass kept on the podium. It always worked as a helpful pause.

"I will request," I said, "that you cooperate with the police. Make sure that violence is stopped because the fire of revenge is never one-sided. *Ab is desh ki shanti aur izzat aapke haaton mein hai.* Now this country's peace, this country's esteem is in your hands. Do not let it down. *Bharat ki jai, bharatvaasion ki jai.*"

Their applause was slow at the start, but it soon gained strength and ended on a high note. I listened to the cheers carefully because they revealed a lot about the effect of my words. It sounded tentative but satisfying.

As the cameras became busy capturing the sea of upraised hands, I noticed a woman. She stood away from a knot of men near the stage. Her pallu was caught between her teeth. She had a girl of about seven years in her arms. The girl was smiling and picking her nose.

I again took a pause, allowing myself another look at them. Then I returned to my chair.

The announcer approached the podium and began showering appreciation for my speech. Gesturing with my fingers, I called Shiva. He stood behind my chair and lowered his ear near my mouth.

"Do you see her?" I asked him in a whisper.

He followed my gaze. "Yes, Sir," he replied.

"I want her."

He glanced at the woman. "The one in a green sari, right, Sir?"

"No," I said, "her daughter."

The girl was still smiling. Watching her white teeth made a part of my body hard, the only organ in me that was not Hindu.

Shiva nodded silently. He was moving away when I called him again.

"One more thing," I said.

"Sir?"

"The next time I visit a gathering and do not receive a garland, it will not end well for you. *Samjhe tum?* And tell them to get a proper chair for me."

"Sorry," he said and went away.

Five minutes later, the announcer invited me to the stage again, saying he would present me with a garland and a bouquet.

Chapter 3

Riju

Hope had poured out through our primary wireless receiver this morning. The South African army had been victorious in locating our position. They were about to despatch a pair of helicopters for our rescue.

But we faced multiple problems. The smoke of the fire would make visibility from the air difficult. Also, the area around us crawled with trees, swamps and dense grass, with no bald patch for landing. A clear place lay several metres from the eastern line of the fire, barely wide enough for one helicopter to land at a time. The army instructed us, "Reach there in half an hour before the fire gets there."

I ran into my tent, my heart thumping. I tossed my mobile phones into my saddlebag; nothing else was as important. Nelson and his fellows were already roaming about the neighbouring tents by the time I got back out. They urged others to come out immediately. They picked up the remaining backpacks on their shoulders.

We hurried towards the rendezvous point. We had decided to stay together, but our group soon split apart because many of us could not run. Professor Victor from France experienced breathing problems two minutes after we started. He disappeared in the tall grasses behind us.

Nelson and the other natives threaded through the bushes, splitting the foliage with experienced hands. They flung away the backpacks, which were slowing down their pace, as they sprinted towards the greenery ahead.

Survival of the fittest depended on the context. The scholars had won several competitions back in their universities. But here in the forest, they were no match for Nelson and his companions. They ran so fast that their dark figures soon vanished into a thicket of trees.

Behind them, Keira and I sprinted ahead of the rest of the group.

A thought about the research drafts that would be left behind crossed my mind, but they could not be saved now. Golden flames twinned like creepers from one tree to another. We found it challenging to know how far or near the fire spread in broad daylight. Nonetheless, the smoke gave us a fair idea. It told us that the fire was no more than five hundred metres away, coming towards us at a fast pace.

"I'm a coward," Keira shouted, running.

"Why do you think so?" I asked her, pausing for her to catch up.

"I'm leaving behind my team."

"What else could you have done?"

Her breaths became faster as she approached me.

"I don't know," she said.

"It's not your fault. You could not have done anything differently."

"No," she said, panting. "There must have been a solution. I could not find it."

She was one of those people who thought that solutions always existed. And their brains brimmed with knowledge – confident of cracking any code. I was not surprised that she did not believe in God.

"You can't control everything that happens around you," I said. "Save yourself if you can-"

I stopped as I heard the clamour of hooves close by. The sound was panicked but still rhythmic. Soon, a flood of black animal bodies, shaking off mud, galloped towards us. They were the African wildebeests. They looked like a cross between a cow and a horse. They must be running away from the fire without knowing they were dashing towards another line of fire.

Deciding to let the scared animals pass by, I stopped Keira, and we ducked behind a fallen log. I watched their long narrow heads flipping sideways as they crossed us. The muscular alpha was followed by other males and females. Behind all of them, a calf sprang ahead with full enthusiasm. It ran fast but somehow still lagged behind.

That's when I noticed it.

Beyond the slick backs of the wildebeests stood an umbrella thorn with its branches spread wide against the sky. Under it lay a pile of stone bricks so small that it was barely distinguishable from the anthills that surrounded it.

There was something strange about the shape of the mound. It looked collapsed, but not quite; dishevelled, but not entirely. The arrangement of the bricks bore the memory of a plan. As if, long back, those rectangular stones had been stacked into a house. A small hut, perhaps.

I stole a glance at Keira. She slowly shook her head as she watched the wildebeests go by. Her face grimaced as she looked stricken by guilt. A failed leader, too preoccupied to notice anything worthwhile.

In an instant, my brain formed a plan.

"Keira," I said. "We must hurry. This way."

She said nothing, picking up a backpack lying nearby on the ground. Saving a few research records might lighten her grief, she must have thought. We then followed the trampled grass which the wildebeests had left in their wake. After jogging around the monstrous trunk of a baobab, we reached a strip of land surrounded by wildflowers.

Nelson and his men were already waiting there. Not for us, for the helicopter.

"I have spent my entire life in this forest," Nelson said with a grin, "but I have never seen a gazelle run behind a hyena before."

Keira gave him a look of disgust. Her tired figure dropped down on the ground.

"You see," Nelson widened his smile, "the fire chased them-"

I held up a hand. "We get it."

Nelson looked at his men and raised his palms as if urging them to utter the question he had in his mind. But the other natives spoke little English.

"When is the helicopter supposed to come?" Nelson asked me.

I checked my watch even though I knew the time. Since the moment I had seen the stone bricks, I had been counting every minute.

"In eleven minutes," I replied.

"We hope it reaches on time."

I was getting impatient. I turned at Keira, whose head was now bowed down between her knees. Perhaps she was crying.

"I will be back in a moment," I said.

She looked up at me with moist eyes. "What do you mean?"

"I'm going back for Professor Victor. What if he is stuck somewhere?"

"No, you are not going anywhere."

"Not all the way back," I assured her. "I will just go till the hillock."

"Don't be ridiculous." She sounded exhausted. "I can't give you permission for this."

"Keira, I am not asking for permission. I will be back in time."

"Don't, please. Okay, wait, one second. Nelson!"

Nelson approached her. When Keira requested him to accompany me, he grinned and went back, standing beside his men.

"Deven," Keira said.

"I will be okay," I said. "Don't wait up for me."

With another look at the fire that was closing in, I left. I had reached the baobab when I met the professors coming from the opposite direction. Professor Murakami led the group. His face was flushed red, sweat dripping from his chin. I told him which way they must go, then hurried away.

I found the fallen log behind which Keira and I had hidden. I heard the sound of the chopper. Its heavy rattles cut through the silence of the forest. Not looking up, I started running towards the umbrella thorn. Clicking pictures of the stone brick mound on my second mobile, I sent it across to a number.

No, not a mound. A hut. From up close, it certainly looked like a small house.

Perhaps the gap through which I entered had been a door centuries ago. Or maybe it had been a window. The inside of the hut smelled of fresh soil, and the floor was overrun with anthills. My fingers slipped across wet moss spread on the walls. A stretch of the sky had replaced the ceiling ages ago.

My heart had been pounding since I had reached here, but now it turned into a more ominous drumroll.

I could not hear the chopper anymore. It must have landed, I thought. Keira and Nelson and Murakami and others must be climbing into it right now. Keira must have asked the pilot if he could wait some more, receiving a reply in the negative.

I remembered my mother, my beautiful, wise mother. She had once told me about Bhagat Singh, who was hung when he was twenty-three. She had said, "While some lives are long, their stories are short, and while some lives are short, their stories are long. What matters is the story, not the life."

I put my life on the line because I trusted the intelligence I had received from the RAW headquarters. Otherwise, I would die thousands of miles away from my mother for nothing.

At once, I began my search for the object.

This ancient dwelling did not have a ceiling; the open sky gazed down. So I started my search at the top halves of the walls, which had collapsed against each other. I pushed my fingers into the gaps left by missing stones. I pulled out the loose blocks but found nothing, not even ants. Perhaps they knew that their homes would soon get burnt, and thus they had fled away.

All the while, I could sense the tick-tick of my wristwatch growing louder and louder. It seemed to fill the background, replacing the trees and the whispers and the forest's colours. As if the sound came not from a tiny device but from the branches clicking against each other outside. It reminded me that my chances of survival kept reducing with the passage of every second.

My stomach felt tight from tension.

After I searched through two walls, I moved to the floor. It was inlaid with stones that had come loose because of age. I pushed them aside and exposed the ground underneath. It crawled with more anthills without inhabitants. I began to dig.

Suddenly there was a crack in the half-silence around me. It made me think of a helicopter flying down towards the forest floor — giant blades slicing the air. The second chopper had arrived. The last chopper. The last drop of hope.

My hands let go of the soil. I sat motionless for a moment on the ground. What should I do? What was the right thing to do? If I had to live, I must go now. Catch the flight. Get transported thousands of miles away. Go home.

Home.

I remembered I did not have a home. Homeland was all that I had.

I did not think of this in a zealously patriotic manner. It was the only way I could think. I did not have a name. I only had a country where no one knew my true identity.

It was supposed to be this way. I had trained alone, without a uniform. I practised inside a soundproof shooting range in Kolkata so that no one would know that I came there. No earplugs, no protective gears, because my trainers said that was how I had to face the world. They wanted to turn me into a simple man and mingle with the crowd. Hence, they converted me into a simple man with extraordinary capabilities. They demanded that I love my country till death, even though my country would refuse to acknowledge my existence even if I was dying.

It was the most extreme form of unrequited love.

The decision now was simple. I had to stay because my job was more precious than my life.

I picked up a twig lying nearby and kept on digging into the ground. After a while, the chopper became silent. It had landed. My fingers were cramping up now, strength draining away from my muscles. My energy was depleted, along with my hopes.

It was then that my fingers bumped against something hard. I stopped digging. Using my hands, I cleared the area. Immediately my eyes widened from disbelief. How unoriginal, I thought, how clichéd — a box buried in the ground.

If the object was what I thought it was, this moment would be forever embossed in history. New chapters would be penned down, and many existing ones would be re-written. Changes would occur in thoughts and theories, facts and figures, beliefs and superstitions.

I stopped my hands from shaking out of excitement as I pulled the box out. My arms could feel its heaviness, the weight of a new era.

The box hardly looked like a box. Roughly carved out of stone, it was ancient and as big as a fat dictionary. Veins of anthills ran across it. I hoped the ants hadn't dug their ways through its contents. Although no lock hung on it, it was sealed. I shook it but heard nothing move inside. The thought of using force to open it crossed my mind, but I was scared of damaging it.

For a moment, I thought faint whirs of the chopper came to my ears. My last hope of survival was leaving. No, *our* last hope. A new history and me. But I had to check if I missed anything here. I dug deeper, ensured that nothing else was concealed in the ground. Then I quickly searched through the remaining walls, dislodging a few bricks. But I found nothing else. As I slipped the package into my backpack, the chopper fired up outside. This time the sound of its wings was clear. My spine grew cold.

I was not going to make it.

Under a blazing sun, I ran in the wilderness towards a blazing fire. Skipping over fallen trees, ducking under branches, I ran. I climbed over the log that had saved Keira and me from the surge of wildebeests. I cried out for help. I almost felt as if the smell of smoke had reached me.

But instead, something else reached me – the sound of the helicopter. They were not going away. Instead, they were coming for me. I looked up wearily and spotted the delightful chopper descending towards me. Nearer, nearer, now sweeping the grass around me. Nearer, growing more enormous, now the pilot's face bleakly visible. But then it did not come down any further, kept on hovering mid-air.

I understood they could not land here. Someone, a blessed soul inside the chopper, threw out a rope ladder at me. I jumped and clung to it. Not forgetting that I was supposed to fake the physical abilities of an average person, I took my time climbing up the ladder. I even accepted Keira's help as she pulled me up through the last couple of steps.

Eight more professors and two army men occupied the helicopter. Professor Victor sat among them, sweating profusely and yet grinning. He was so happy upon seeing me that he tried to rise but could not because he was strapped to his seat.

"How did you reach, Professor?" I asked him, raising my voice over the drone of the chopper.

He cupped his hands on the sides of his mouth and shouted, "I was lucky. I found a shortcut."

I smiled, then looked at Keira.

"Professor, I had requested you not to wait."

"Told," she said, "not 'requested'."

"Yes, told. So?"

She shrugged.

"Thank you," I said, smiling.

She nodded once in reply and pointed at the backpack on my lap. "You can keep it down on the floor. There is enough space."

"It is okay," I said, clutching onto it.

The earth dropped below us outside, taking all dangers farther and farther away. As the threat to my life subsided, I stopped myself from thinking about the mysterious artefact in my bag. I allowed myself a little time and reflected on the scenery.

Unlike those in the dazzlingly green forests back in India, the trees here stood apart. Most of them were brown in colour with sprinkles of green leaves this time of the year. Less hiding space made the sightings of animals easier. I had seen so many deers that I had grown tired of it. One of the most exciting incidents happened right behind our last camp a few weeks back. A cheetah had chased a gazelle towards another cheetah that had been waiting behind the bushes. I had felt bad for the deer, but nature never ceased to take its natural course.

From memories, I shifted my focus to the fire. The two separate lines of forest fire were actually the arms of a vast semicircle. I saw a river where the semicircle ended. That meant the only hope the trapped animals had of surviving was swimming across the water. From up here, the fire appeared to progress slowly, gentle smoke rising from it.

"Where are we going?" Keira asked one of the army men, a native.

"To the camp at Sandriver near Skukuza."

Sandriver was the headquarters of the Kruger National Park Commandos before they were phased out.

"I thought we were flying to Johannesburg," I said.

"We will have you rested for a few hours at the camp," another army man said. "Our Government's personnel will take it from there."

I felt nervousness wrestling with my breaths. I hoped they would not ask me to open my bag and show its contents at the camp.

If they did, my mask would fall off.

Chapter 4

Vikram

The office of the Prime Minister of India was decked up with wooden furniture shiny as glass. His table was heavily lacquered mahogany. It barely rose to the waist of the man sitting behind it. But that did not mean that Suryajit Prasad was tall. He liked perching on high chairs.

He had a square face, an authoritative chest, and eyes that always gave the impression that he had things in control. He switched from spectacles to contact lenses once he won the post three years ago. Eye contact was as important as posture in politics.

He drank tea from a porcelain cup.

"Yesterday, a reporter came to my office," he began, "and asked me if this was green tea or cow's urine."

"He was going for the Hindu-angle," I said. "However, I have heard they are good for your health."

"They?"

"Both of them. Green tea and cow's urine. What did you tell the reporter?"

"My position stops me from using any bad words, although many of them came to my mind right then."

"I hope your party members had the same level of restraint," I told him.

"Oh, so you heard," he said. "Babu Tiwari has no idea how much his statement hurt us yesterday."

"Did you call him up?"

"I could not find the time," he shrugged. "So I sent Sushant to calm him down. You know what Babu said? He said I should not worry because I still have two years left in this first term. Such a fool."

I smiled. "What are we waiting for? I know you dislike starting with small talks."

"I have asked Intisarji to join. She is a part of this. She deserves to know the progress."

I leant in closer to him. "I still don't understand why you involved Intisar. If you put a foot wrong, she will tear you apart in front of the whole country."

"That is why, Rathoreji, I want her to take every step with me in this."

"Everyone thinks she is the most aggressive opposition leader this country has ever seen."

"She is formidable, I admit. Her ideas might be misplaced, but when it comes to delivering speeches, her only competitor is you."

There was a knock on the door. Balwinder Singh, the head clerk of the Prime Minister, entered.

"Madam Intisar Khan is here, Sir."

"Please let her come in," Suryajit said. "Oh, Singhji, I forgot to ask you before. Did your child get the admission?"

Balwinder paused for a moment, then nodded.

"In which school?" Suryajit asked.

"Sir...Sir...," the clerk kneaded his hands together, hesitating. "Skywalk International School."

Suryajit gave him a slight smile. "It's okay if you send your daughter to a private school. There is nothing to hesitate."

"Yes, okay, yes, Sir."

"I want *motichoor ke laddus*, Singhji," I said.

Balwinder's shoulders loosened as he nodded in relief. I watched him leave and then turned back to Suryajit, who remained quiet. He picked up a pen from his desk and began clicking it on and off.

"Education," he said softly into the air between us, "education, education, education."

I stayed silent. I did not ask Suryajit to which school he would have sent his child if he had one because I knew his principles were more robust than the system he wanted to repair.

The tall, stunning Intisar Khan walked in through the door. She carried the elegance which her family had perfected through generations of serving in politics. Her parents had been eminent leaders, holding key positions in different states at various times. Her grandfather was the founder of Insaaf Dal. The party took merely one decade to become a formidable force in India. A white *chikankari* dupatta covered Intisar's head.

"Good morning, gentlemen," every word was valued in her British-schooled English pronunciation. "This is my daughter, Aziza."

Aziza was around twenty-five and as graceful as her mother. She was slimmer than Intisar. The way she followed her mother spoke of a detached upbringing. I stopped looking at her, conscious of not staring for too long.

At first, I thought with bitterness that the Khan family had made the same mistake again. They had not introduced another family member to poverty. Perhaps that was why they could never rise to power at the centre. The poor did not vote for them. Or maybe the poor were jealous of their wealth and ended up electing a competitor.

It happened in politics. In politics, everything happens.

"I hope it is alright if I join you," Aziza said.

"Of course, it is alright," Intisar said, then looked at Suryajit. "She completed her PhD in Political Science from JNU last year. Now she serves as a junior member of our party."

"I did not know that Insaaf Dal took interns," I said.

"*Janab*, she is not an intern," Intisar explained. "She is a full-time member."

"Even then, I think this is not the right classroom for a *yuva karyakarta*."

"Rathoreji is right," Suryajit told Intisar. "We should keep this secret for as long as possible."

"Pardon me, but I don't agree with you," Aziza said, with not even a tremble in her voice. "Our objective here involves the interest of the country and the world. This matter should be opened up to the public at once."

"I see," Suryajit said. "So you have the same thoughts as your mother. Intisarji, I am sorry, but I have my reservations against including anyone new at this stage."

"*Janab*," Intisar said in a polite tone, "please understand, your higher position in the system does not automatically make you the sole decision-maker here. I am travelling outside the country next week and will not be available for a few days. In my absence, Aziza will represent me in this group."

Suryajit looked at me for a moment, then turned to Aziza. "In that case, you can join us, Aziza. But please know that this mission will be kept a secret for now. We had decided it in the beginning."

Aziza did not give a reply. She took a seat beside me, and her mother sat down on her other side. I found the smell of rose attar coming from the girl arousing.

"Here is the update," Suryajit said. "Our man is alive. He is coming back."

"Thank God," I said. "Thank God."

"We have rerouted his flight to New Delhi via Mumbai for avoiding suspicions," the Prime Minister added. "He will reach here today evening."

"Does he have the…?" Intisar asked.

"Yes."

"Re-consider what we are doing," Intisar said to Suryajit, "what we have done. If the word goes out, our country's reputation will be ruined."

"I think the time of decision has passed," I said.

"I still believe we must be open about it to the world," Aziza insisted. "It is not just about our country. When others know about it, which they will eventually, they will feel betrayed."

"We will make them understand the reasons behind our discretion," I said.

"It is not that simple," Intisar said.

"What do you mean?" Suryajit asked her.

"We know this is a critical moment for India," Aziza replied on behalf of her mother. "With uncertain Governments in America and Pakistan and the brewing chemistry between China and Pakistan, the power dynamics are shifting."

I thought, sniffing more rose fragrance, this girl was reading too many textbooks. She might even blurt out that world politics was all about gaining and losing bargaining power.

"There is growing distrust in the neighbourhood. Even Nepal is-" she stopped, perhaps realizing she was going out of context. "My fear is, once we announce that we have the object, sharks from everywhere will close in on us."

"Hmm, I understand your concern," Suryajit said patiently. "Rathoreji?"

"It depends on how we disclose it," I said. "And how much."

"Are you suggesting partial secrecy?" Intisar asked, raising her eyebrows.

"No," I said, "misinformation. We might tell the world that we had no idea how crucial and precious the object was."

Intisar lifted a hand, then let it fall down on her lap. She shook her head.

"*Aur zarurat padi,*" she said, "*toh galti bhi maan lenge, hai na?*"

"With all due respect," Aziza glanced at me, "this idea is ridiculous."

I looked at her, at her brave face. One day this girl would shift her eyes outside libraries and classrooms and see the happenings around us. She would realize the reality. This blind Muslim girl thought we would be the only country to feed the world lies.

"With all due respect," I said calmly, "without your mother, you have no idea how long it would have taken you to step foot into this office."

Her stare aroused me even more.

"No," Suryajit said before Intisar could start defending her daughter, "Rathoreji, I think she is right. Let's not take chances that might backfire."

"So you intend to tell everyone the truth and then deal with the consequences?"

"Not just the truth. The whole truth. I will tell people why we had to keep this a secret. I know it will attract a flurry of criticisms, but we have proofs backing our statements."

"Which proofs?" I asked.

"I have not seen them yet," Suryajit said. "But Venkat said we have enough evidence."

I ran a few quick thoughts in my head. "Fine. I have faith in your decision."

"So let us gather again in the evening," the Prime Minister said. "Thank you all for coming."

Intisar rose from her chair.

"By the way," I said. "Where is Venkat? I thought he would join us."

"He's making arrangements for the arrival of our man," Suryajit said. "The chief of the RAW loves to be on the field."

"No wonder his shaven head has acquired a strong tan," I said, smiling.

Chapter 5

Riju

At the Sandriver camp, six officials wearing black coats arrived for receiving us. It was a stroke of luck that the officials took us to the Johannesburg army headquarters without inspecting our luggage and asked us to rest. But a break was the last thing in my mind. I told them it would be great if I could leave right away. Thankfully, all the foreign professors also longed for returning to their respective countries without delay. It had been a tiresome exploration, and although at the end of it they had not achieved their goal, they were happy to be still alive.

Only I knew that not all of us had failed. Perhaps, someday in the future, a few of my teammates would look back at this incident and realize why I did what I did. But it was a far cry. I am doomed to go down in their memories as a person who broke their trust, a backstabber.

At the Johannesburg airport, my heart turned cold as I proceeded for luggage check-in. If they came to know about the package in my backpack, I was finished. I would be caught, and even my own country would label me as a shame. As I walked ahead, the thin corridor leading up to the customs seemed narrower, almost suffocating. The ceiling gave the impression of slanting lower and lower.

Panicked, frantic, I began to think of an alternate escape route. Then one of the officials accompanying us approached me. He asked for my passport. I touched my pocket and realized I had a magic wand – a maroon diplomatic passport could work wonders. As soon as I gave it to the man, he rushed us through a security-free way.

Freedom was often associated with things that had nothing to do with it. For me, it was the specially arranged South African Airlines flight from Johannesburg to Mumbai via Abu Dhabi. Once I reached my destination, I mingled with the crowd. After that, the journey from Mumbai to New Delhi was a quick hop.

I did not expect Venkat, my chief, the mastermind of the RAW, to receive me at the New Delhi airport. I was right – no one turned up. I caught a pre-booked taxi. Somehow the driver knew that I had a booking at hotel Chand Bahaar in Tooti Chowki. Not surprisingly, he was also aware that I was required at the All India Institute of Medical Sciences in two hours. Of course, he reminded me, I should not forget my backpack that had my medical reports.

"Which medical reports?" I asked him.

"These." He handed me an envelope containing a sheaf of papers.

I began flipping through them. "An undercover cop should not look like a cop," I told him.

"I am not a policeman."

"Then who are you?"

"You are suffering from chronic knee pain," the man said. "That's what the reports say." He left.

The meeting, the handover, would happen in the evening. It would not take place at the office of the Prime Minister. It was too risky.

A couple of hours later, I entered an X-ray chamber of the AIIMS hospital and found four people already sitting inside. On the left was Vikram Rathore, his formidable figure barely fitting into a small chair. Beside him sat the Prime Minister, and the others present were Intisar Khan and a young woman I had not seen before.

"Venkat wanted to be the middleman in this matter," the Prime Minister said, "but I thought of receiving the parcel directly from you."

"I did not see any security outside, Sir," I said.

"Then the security has done a wonderful job," Suryajit said. "And please don't call me 'Sir'. I am a man of the people."

"Alright," I said.

He leant forward. "And 'the people' also includes you. It makes me greatly uncomfortable that I can't thank you and all others involved in this operation from a stage, before everyone. The common people will never know of your bravery, but the legacy of bravery will always remember you."

"I agree," Vikram nodded his head. "All of us are very grateful to you."

Intisar looked at Suryajit. *"Janab* has at least acknowledged the importance of being transparent. Anyway," she turned towards me, "I know your mission became way more dangerous than expected. We are so happy to see you unharmed."

"Thank you," I said.

"I am Aziza, her daughter," the young woman said, tilting her head towards Intisar. "Your actions surpassed your duty. We are proud of you." She smiled.

I picked the backpack from the floor and gave it to Suryajit. Perhaps more flourish would have been appropriate for the act, but I longed to get over with this final part of the mission.

The room slipped into silence as the Prime Minister unzipped the bag and looked inside. I had not even cleaned the package, merely covered it with brown paper. Dust accumulations often reveal a lot about age and the surroundings. I could have by accident removed a trace of DNA.

"I see that you did not take off its lid," Suryajit said to me.

"You did the right thing," Vikram said. "We need to be careful while opening it. The contents inside must not be disturbed."

"Should we open it at all?" Aziza questioned. "Or should we wait till our suspicions clear up, then deliver it in its original form to the United Nations?"

I thought the query was valid, but no one considered it worth a reply.

"How does it feel, Mr Prime Minister?" Intisar asked. "The shape of history in your hands."

"Only time will tell if it is the shape of history or the future, Intisarji. Now we must find a reliable person who can keep this box without damaging it. You have anyone in mind?"

Intisar opened her mouth to reply, but Vikram cut in.

"Dr Tharoor would be an appropriate person for the job," he said. "He is a specialist in outer-space debris inspection at the BARC. And he has shown before that he can keep government secrets buried."

"Dr Tharoor," Suryajit said. "Hmm. He is a veteran. Good suggestion."

"So right now," Aziza said, "who would take its responsibility? Riju, you?"

I shook my head. "I am going to Basirhat, my home town, for Durga puja, if I get permission from my chief. I do not think it would be smart to carry the parcel there. Besides, I have little idea of what's inside, of its importance."

"I thought you have a fair idea," Aziza said, puzzled. "Were you not detailed about it before the project started?"

"Often, the briefing sessions of intelligence operations are neither complete nor correct," I said. "Many a time, we go in search of gold dust and end up finding sand."

"If no one has any problem, I can keep it," Intisar offered, "till Dr Tharoor comes and gets it."

"Oh," Vikram said, "but you will be leaving for a foreign trip shortly. We should find someone who can keep a close watch on it all the time."

"*Janab*, I do not prefer you calling it a 'trip'. It is a ministry-related visit, but I get your point. I can have it postponed. However, I don't want to raise any suspicion."

"I am attending the Global Environment Summit day after tomorrow," Suryajit said. "Azizaji, can you-"

"*Koi baat nahin*," Vikram said, "let me take its responsibility. I will have to make a few changes to my schedule, but that will not be a problem."

"Fine," Suryajit said, relieved, "it is decided then. Please take Dr Tharoor into confidence before handing the box over."

"If you face any problem," Aziza told Vikram, "inform me. I will be available for help."

"We might need to gather again as soon as we get any news from Rathoreji," Suryajit said.

The meeting ended. All of us stood up. I extended a hand to the Prime Minister, who, instead of accepting it, pulled me into an embrace and congratulated me. Smiles were directed at each other, and parting wishes were exchanged. Although, I could sense the tension in the air as no one mentioned any kind of celebration. Perhaps we knew this was the beginning of a greater struggle, a mighty step that could never be retraced.

At the door, I asked Intisar, "How are we going to spread the news across the world?"

She looked at Suryajit as if daring him to answer me.

"We are still figuring out that part," the Prime Minister replied. "One more thing. I am permitting you to visit your hometown. You deserve a holiday."

"Thank you," I said, "but without the permission of my chief, I can't go anywhere."

"I see," he said with a smile. "Alright, I will talk to Venkat."

Aziza and I exited the room after everyone else had left. "So even the Prime Minister's permission is not sufficient for you?" she asked me in the empty corridor.

I smiled. "Each operator is a bug walking on a spider's web. One wrong move by any one of us can create unwanted ripples."

"I understand. By the way, I am also visiting Basirhat for Muharram, which will be celebrated the day after Durga puja this year. I will stay with my grandfather. If you are free for a meeting, give me a call."

I gave her a nod. We reached the end of the corridor.

"Interesting word, 'operator'", she said softly. "For some reason, I have always disliked the word 'spy'."

I placed a finger on my lips, gesturing her to keep quiet on the matter.

Chapter 6

Vikram

On the margin of Basirhat in West Bengal stood a small house. In the heart of that house was a small room. And inside the room sat a woman without her daughter. She could not find her child for the past two days. Perhaps the woman had cried and cried, then knocked on several doors asking for help. Did anyone agree to help her? I did not know.

In the middle of Malabar Hills in Mumbai stood an enormous bungalow. In its heart was a big room, and inside the room sat a girl without her mother. She was locked in. She had not cried even once since she had been brought here. She had screamed on the first night but had soon realized it was a waste of energy. After a spell of refusing food, she understood it would not make her situation any better. She wanted the person who brought her here to think she was brave, but her trembling lips gave her away.

Would anyone come to help the girl? No. This I knew because the bungalow belonged to me.

The girl from Basirhat sat on the edge of the bed, a white teddy bear in her lap. She was beautiful, her cheeks carrot-coloured, but now her face looked drawn and somehow older. Surely her eyes would have sparkled had she not been upset. However, at present, dark shadows spread in them. Her delicate fingers dug into the teddy's fur, and below her frock, her knee caps rose prominently. It seemed unthinkable that this harsh world could accommodate such a fragile being.

I kneeled down before her, raised her chin with my hand.

"What is your name?" I asked her.

She remained silent.

"*Aapka naam kya hai?*" I repeated.

She moved her lips but made no sound.

"If you speak to me, I will take you to your mom."

At the mention of her mother, her eyeballs trembled, and a sudden breath escaped her mouth.

"*Sacchi?*" she asked and lifted her little finger.

"*Main aapse vada karta hun,*" I said.

"My name is Noor," she said. The pout she made while pronouncing her name remained on her lips even afterwards.

"Noor," I said, "do you know the story of Noor Jahan?"

She moved her little finger from left to right, gesturing 'no'.

"What is your name?" she asked.

"I am Vikram."

"His name is Baadshah," she patted the teddy.

"Noor, I will take you back to your mother."

A wide grin appeared on her face, and out of happiness, her legs kicked the air.

"Can we go now, please?"

"Sadly, we are very far from your home. So we must make some preparations before we step out. Understood?"

"But uncle did not make any preparation before making me leave home? He did not even tell me why we came here."

"Uncle is a fool," I said. "He even forgot to bring your mother with you."

"Uncle is a fool," she pouted dramatically. "I don't like him."

"That is why I came here. So, can we begin our arrangements?"

She made her teddy bear nod with her hands, suggesting 'yes'.

"First of all," I said, "we will let your mother know that you are alright. And to do it, we will send her a video."

"A video?" Her eyes widened from excitement.

"Yes." I brought out my mobile phone. I placed the device on a table, starting the recording with the camera facing us. Noor pushed her little finger into her nose, then took it out.

"*Ammijaan*," she screamed at the camera, "*ammi, main bilkul theek hun*. This uncle, uncle Vikram will bring me-"

"No," I stopped her, "not like this. You can't just say that you are alright. You must prove it to *ammi*."

"What do you mean?"

"How would she know that you are telling the truth?"

"Owww. Right, right." She made the teddy nod again. "Umm, how should I make her understand that I am fine?"

"She will know that you are alright if you can recite something for her."

"Recite *matlab*?"

"Tell her something that you have read in a book, maybe."

"Can I recite her a poem?"

"Yes, you can. You surely can. But you can say something even better."

"What?"

I touched her shoulder and said, "A few lines from the Koran."

She turned silent. Looking around the room, she bit her lips, engrossed in thought.

"There is a problem," she told me at last. "I don't know any line from the Koran."

"That is not true," I said, taken aback. "Have you forgotten it?"

She shook Baadshah's head.

"I have never read it," she said. "Even many of my cousins have never read it."

"Noor, please, no joking."

"I am not joking."

"But- but you are a Muslim."

"That is correct. My *abbu* was a Muslim. My *ammi* is a Muslim. Salman, my brother, he is also a Muslim. We are Muslims."

Her childish antics irritated me.

"Every Muslim is supposed to read the Koran and remember its words," I said.

She kept quiet and chewed her lips again.

I felt impatience growing hotter in me. "Maybe *ammi* has taught you a paragraph?"

"*Ammi*," she began to sob. "I want *ammi. Ammijaan.*"

"We will meet her, *bachhi.* Stop crying now. We will go to *ammi.*"

I had not expected this. I had thought that the first thing Muslim parents taught their children was how to be a Muslim. A pure, proper Muslim. Muslim girls, since childhood, had to wear *burqas* and study at an Islamic school, I had assumed. I did not have much knowledge of what else they did. I never went into the depths of their customs for fear of getting sucked into it. I saw its surface and found it ugly. Oh, another thing. Muslims also trained their children to hate Hindus, didn't they? Indeed they fed the theories of me versus you, Allah against Vishnu, my ways clashing with your ways. The superiority of my devotion over yours.

In the end, Gods fought with each other through their believers.

Noor's complete ignorance of Muslim traditions baffled me.

"Do you visit the mosque?" I asked her.

Her face brightened at once. "Yes, *ammi* and I go to the masjid in our neighbourhood. There I play with Abdul *chacha*. When he bows down for prayer, I climb on his back and turn him into my horse. He does not mind. He does not get disturbed."

I saw a flicker of hope. "Noor, *bachhi,* do you pray? Do you sit for namaz?"

The girl did not speak.

"How do you pray then?" I asked.

"When I want to reach Allah," she said, "I speak to Him through my thoughts. If I need anything, I say it quietly. I once secretly had a popsicle and prayed that I don't catch a cold. And I did not."

"You don't sit for namaz?"

"Un-huh," she shook her head. "*Ammi* does. She asks me to join her sometimes. But she does not force me. And when she goes for work, our house becomes empty." She looked down at the teddy. "Can we take Baadshah with us, please?"

"Of course," I replied. "Noor, it is very important for you to inform *ammi* that you are alright. And for that, you must recite from the Koran. You must sit for namaz. You should wear a burqa. Until you do these, *ammi* will keep on worrying for you."

"I am a bad girl. I am good for nothing."

"Don't cry now, don't."

She raised her face at me, her nose running. "Can you recite the Koran?"

Even the thought of it made me cringe. Fire rushed in my veins, and my throat felt hot.

"No," I said, "I can't."

"Then?" She simpered. "You should also learn it. I want *ammi*."

"We will find a way," I said, patting the side of her head. "Now you eat and go to sleep. *Achhi bachhi.* I will be back."

I left her and entered my bedroom. I rang up Shiva's phone and asked him to meet me. He appeared before me.

"There is a problem," I told Shiva. "The girl has not read the Koran. She does not sit for namaz."

"Maybe her mother is too busy, Sir. But why is it a problem?"

"If she does not act like a Muslim girl, we can't shoot the video."

He scratched his head for a moment. "I have a solution. It is easy."

"Tell me."

"What if, when we shoot the video, we make her wear a burqa?" he said. "We can keep the Koran open in front of her, and she can read from it. We will make her sit down on her knees."

"No, Shiva, you are not understanding. If the girl is not Muslim enough, I can't hate her enough. If I can't hate her enough, I can't hurt her. And hurting her is the main point of all this."

"Please don't mind," he raised a pair of curious eyebrows, "but why can't you hurt her if you don't hate her?"

"Don't talk rubbish, please. Have you seen the girl's face? Have you heard the way she talks? She is a plain innocent child."

"Maybe you can try acting."

"*Tum chup raho,*" I said. "Let me think."

"I am sorry, Sir. No matter what, we can't let her go now. She might talk."

"Let me think, please."

Shiva turned to leave.

"There is a way," I called behind him, "Shiva."

"Sir?"

"You have to teach her quotes from the Koran. Make her wear a burqa regularly. Take her to a mosque, but be careful when you step out with her."

"But what if she refuses to learn?"

"She won't refuse," I assured him. "Tell her that if she learns to do these activities, her *ammi* will love her more. And tell her once she is ready, she can go home and meet her mother."

"Which will be a lie again."

I nodded.

"But it will not happen in one day," he said. "People can get suspicious. The longer we keep her here, the riskier it will become for us."

"No problem, I will wait. Shiva, we must not forget our aim. Noor is the seed of her community. She will achieve something that she would never have accomplished in her whole life. And we will make her do it."

"I was thinking about it last night, Sir. It is actually straightforward. We are about to hurt her because she is a Muslim."

I looked at him. His body, huge as a mountain, was capable of mere physical force. His idiotic brain did not know that the best way of defeating an army was to make it clash with a more enormous army, a minority against a majority. One must drive the enemy mad enough to fight a battle even they knew they could never win.

"Noor is a Muslim," I said, "true, but she is also Lord Shiva, the God of creation and destruction. A child has more power than anyone else to create and destroy."

Shiva gave me a look of respect that rose out of confusion. I did not blame him. He was an uncomplicated man, and my words were becoming more cryptic.

"For now, do as I say," I told him. "Train the girl into a *pukka* Muslim. You can go now."

He began to walk away but then turned back and asked where to put the artefact from South Africa. I instructed him to lock it up in the almirah.

Chapter 7

Riju

With Venkat's permission, I reached Basirhat. In a brightly coloured pandal on one side of our locality, we worshipped Maa Durga. The last five days of the puja were filled with joyous celebrations. The Navratris ended, and Vijaya Dashami arrived before I could prepare myself for it. Today She would return to the mythical Kailasha, where Her husband Lord Shiva waited.

In the morning, a few women put sweetmeat on Her lips. They smeared vermillion along the parting of Her hair, daubed some more on Her cheeks. They danced to the rhythm of *dhaaks* and rubbed vermillion onto each other, sprinkling it like *gulaal* during Holi. Soon their faces and their white saris were covered in red. After the final chanting of mantras, Maa was ready for the journey. I joined my neighbours for the procession from Basirhat to Taki. We carried Maa to the bank of the Ichamati, where thousands of people had gathered.

The marvellous spectacle began under the large, slanted eyes of Maa Durgas, who came from all parts of West Bengal. As the wind blew across the border of India and Bangladesh, colourful lights blinked on both sides of Ichamati, even while the sun was still out. In the river, water was barely visible, for its surface was crammed with boats. Boats of different sizes, many of them tied together, were ready to carry the idols.

Throngs of Indians cheered on the near side of the river. Crowds of Bangladeshis jostled crazily on the opposite side.

Trucks and hand-pulled vans appeared on both the banks, with Maa covered in smokes that rose from smouldering coconut husks in clay vessels. Women folded their hands and closed their eyes in reverence while a group of children broke into a dance. Numerous Durgas stood tall in a sea of upturned heads.

Soon we shifted our Durga onto three boats fixed together. The boatmen, wearing *lungis* up to their thighs, pushed at the shores with long canes. We began to slide away. I chose a spot near one tip of a boat and sat down.

"Wait," a woman's voice came from the bank. The next second, someone jumped into the boat.

"Please, let me pass," the voice said. "Excuse me, excuse me, thank you."

Aziza's pink sari was draped in the traditional Bengali way. She made her way towards my end of the boat and sat down on a plank beside me.

"What are you doing here?" I raised my voice over the noise of people around us.

"I am following you," she replied with a grin.

"No, you are not."

"How do you know?"

I lowered my voice, "I know it when I am being followed. Are you here for Durga puja?"

"My grandfather lives in Taki. This year he has reserved the guest house for me so that I can also enjoy this." She gestured with her hands towards the surroundings.

"When is-"

I was interrupted as another vessel gently bumped against our boat.

"When is Muharram?" I asked Aziza.

"Tomorrow," she answered. "Where are you coming from?"

"Basirhat."

"You have your own home there?"

"Yes and no."

"What do you mean?"

I threw a look around me. Everyone was busy celebrating.

"People think it is my home. But it is not."

After a few minutes, she leapt up from her seat all of a sudden.

"*Bolo Dugga Maai ki*," she shouted, throwing her hands up in the air. The accent in her Bengali pronunciation was pardonable. Several voices replied in unison, "*Joi!*"

"*Bolo Dugga Maai ki...*"

"Joi!"

"Aschhe bochor abar hobe," she said. "It will happen again next year."

"Bochor bochor egiye jabe," the others replied in unison, "It will keep on happening every year."

"Aschhe bochor abar hobe."

"Bolo Dugga Maai ki…"

"Joi!"

"Joi Maa!"

Everyone cheered for the return of Maa next year and the year after that. They revelled in the hope of tomorrow, in the repetition of happiness that life offered.

Our boats moved across the river, veering away before touching the Bangladeshi bank.

"If the stories I've heard are true," I told Aziza, "long back, people were allowed to get off the boat on this side, but the BSFs stopped it because of illegal crossing. Are you not going to study the refugee problem here?"

She shook her head. "It is a moment of celebration." Although, her face grew serious.

"Come on," I insisted, "tell me."

"Alright," she said at last. "Wherever I go, I can't stop myself from thinking about all the problems people go through. All the issues they have to face and bear with daily."

"So, are you worried all the time?"

"I won't call them worries," she said. "I am concerned about the people on the one hand. But on the other hand, those same thoughts somehow make me feel every issue is an opportunity to improve."

Our boats made seven circles in the water. Every time we neared the other side of the river, the Bangladeshis who stood on the bank threw small gifts into our boats. *Gamchas,* conch shells, and other tokens of good wishes.

Finally, our boats came back to the middle of the river. We ululated in chorus while lowering our Durga into the water. The golden ribbons that decorated Her floated as She descended slowly; first, Her body, then Her shoulders. Water gathered around her face while She looked up towards the sunset sky. There went her cheeks, the tip of her nose, and with a soft slush, She disappeared.

We also immersed Her weapons. She had ridden Her lion; She had killed Mahisashura, the mighty demon; She had blessed us all. And now She would meet her husband. In the end, only her golden crown and a few marigolds remained on the water, drifting away.

Later in the evening, Aziza and I occupied two chairs on the roof of the Taki guest house, which overlooked the Ichamati. The river sparkled under the moonlight.

"Is it why you joined politics?" I asked her. "Because you feel guilty when you see others in trouble?"

"Yes," she said. "But there are many people who misunderstand my motivation. They think I joined politics because I belong to the Khan family."

"They don't know you. But people have seen your parents and grandparents, and their achievements. For you, it must feel weird, serving the people who don't quite get you."

"That's okay," she said. "As long as I can bring equality, empower the… oh look at me, getting into all this now. Tell me about yourself. How did you get into this?"

"Sorry, I can't."

"Not even a word?" she shook her head. "See, I already know who you are."

"Fine," I said. "My entry was not planned. An operator-"

"You mean an agent?"

"You can call him anything," I said. "A certain person was on a certain mission in a certain country. His secrecy was compromised, so he had to be replaced. His superiors came to the Police Academy searching for a replacement and found me suitable."

"What happened to the man whose place you took?"

"No one ever saw him."

"God," her eyes became large. "Does it happen often, people disappearing?"

I shrugged.

"I once saw this movie," she said, breaking a smile. "There, the, umm, operator falls in love and flees with his lover. And his employers keep chasing him."

"The reality is different," I said. "On the ground, the assignments are not always glamorous or eventful. We are normal people with...I think I should stop here."

"One more question, please. What was the toughest challenge you had to face?"

"Coming to terms with my first alternate identity. It took a while."

She dwelled on it for a moment. "So now, the person that I am talking to – is he the real person or an alternate?"

I remained quiet. I could not explain to Aziza how strange it felt – being someone else. Growing a new skin over your skin. I could not describe how sometimes I felt like I was betraying people who did nothing wrong, like Keira Marshal. And the handful of individuals who knew my truth, even they were wary of trusting me. Even my superiors were aware that double agents were not mythical creatures. They existed in reality.

"You don't need to answer that." Aziza gave me a smile, and a tiny scar beside one of her brown eyes deepened. A slight bump ran down the middle of her forehead, which somehow made her look more endearing. I took my eyes off her, watched the river.

"It does not matter," I said. "I am not the same person I was a few months ago. And I have no idea who I will become next year."

"I am sorry. I ask too many questions. The thing is, I do not like secrets. Which is why, when the Prime Minister decided against telling the public about-"

She stopped as Deenu, the house-help, appeared with our dinner. He had an old radio slung around his neck, from which Birendra Krishna Bhadra recited the Mahisasura Mardini verses. Aziza told Deenu that she loved listening to it. So he left the radio on the table and went away. Even though Mahalaya was long gone, Birendra Krishna Bhadra's yearning voice never sounded odd.

When I was beginning to think this was how the rest of the day would pass, there was a commotion down below. Aziza and I rushed to the railing. A group of six men were quarrelling with the gatekeeper under a street light. The men carried bamboo sticks in their hands. One of them suddenly grabbed the gatekeeper by his neck and started to shout.

"Whoever took our daughter has to pay," he screamed furiously. "They have to pay!"

He brought out something metallic from his back. It was a cleaver.

Chapter 8

Vikram

---

*"T*his is the way the world ends,"* wrote T. S. Eliot, *"not with a bang but a whimper."* A gradual silent death was in store for us all. Our breaths would get weaker and weaker with every passing day till the very end. But what about the *birth* of the universe? It was not quiet. It happened with a boom.

The Big Bang.

Radical changes began in similar ways. More so in a country like India. In this nation, there was no point in being subtle. Nothing about this country was delicate. Extreme poverty stared us in the eye, child mortality rates punched us in the guts, and malnutrition kicked us in the crotch. Huge gaps existed between income levels. With their melodrama, self-obsession, and biases, even the Bollywood cinemas had nothing refined about them.

So when Hindustan was slipping towards darkness, what were we supposed to do? When religious minorities were slow-poisonously becoming more powerful, what must be done? When the children of Mughal invaders were finding their voices, how was rebirth possible?

We needed a boom. To catch people's attention, we had to set off explosions. Hence, my mission was crucial to the origin of the new nation.

I at first thought of taking Noor to Haji Ali. The lonely white mosque stood in the middle of the sea, connected to land by a passage like an umbilical cord. But I had gone there several times. I had distributed alms to the beggars who lay on both sides of the path. I had escorted delegates of the Middle East; before they arrived, those same beggars were kicked away. The problem was that many people knew me there.

The imam, the old singer, and the women who fed the pigeons every day – I could not risk them noticing me with Noor. The girl's picture would soon appear in every news channel and newspaper. She would be the face of a new history. It would be dangerous if people saw me with her. Also, Shiva could not do it because Noor was not yet comfortable with him. After all, he took her away from her mother.

So instead, Noor and I visited the Andheri Chakala mosque. Here no one would recognize me. It was evening, and we sat on a platform outside. Noor extended her arms to see if the sleeves of her new burqa ended exactly at her wrists. She stood up, then sat down, appraising the fitting of her attire. She smiled at me, her lips bright orange from the *rava halwa* she had gobbled a minute back.

"Did you like this mosque?" I asked her.

"This is shinier than *ammi's* burqa," she said, running her fingers across a golden embroidery. "I love it."

"And the mosque?"

She nodded elaborately. She took a deep breath and looked around as if searching for a fragrance she had lost.

"Rose," she said, and again the pout remained on her lips.

"So when Shiva uncle asks you, "Noor, what did you see in the mosque?" what will you say?"

"I will not tell him anything."

"But he has never seen a mosque. He might be curious."

"That is his problem," she said.

"Why, are you not excited to tell him?"

"He did not bring *ammi* with me."

"I agree," I said. "But Shiva uncle is the one who is going to take you back to *ammi*."

"Why can't you come? *Ammi* will like you."

"Okay, I will also come. But I don't know the way to your home. Only Shiva uncle knows. He will guide us."

"Oh," she said, disappointed.

"What will you tell uncle about this mosque?"

She flapped down the veil of her burqa over her face, then threw it back over her head again.

"I will tell him that the imam smells of jasmine," she said. "And that Arabic words are written on the walls. And that you forgot to bring a handkerchief, so you had to buy one for covering your head."

"Good," I nodded appreciatively. "Excellent, Noor. And, what else?"

"I will tell him about the small girl whose hair was orange here and there, just like mine. She sat on the stairs and asked for money. And her *ammijaan*... oh, oh look at those cones tied to that tower."

"They are microphones," I explained. "You heard the *aazaan*, didn't you-"

"*Allah hu Akbar Allah...*" she began to sing, her lips pouting towards the sky.

"Yes, very good. That prayer came out through those cones for everyone to hear."

She drew out a Parle-G biscuit from her pocket and fed it to a pariah dog. The animal ate it and wagged its tail. She then looked towards her left.

"Rose," she said, grinning. Then, she jumped up on her feet. "Can I get a scent, please?" She pointed at an attar shop on the other side of the street.

I could see the shop clearly; hence there was no risk involved.

"Here, take this," I gave her a hundred rupee note. "Don't forget to bring back the change."

She studied the note, turning it over, a glow of wonder appearing on her face. She skipped away. I kept my eyes fixed on her back as she neared the attar shop, her feet moving awkwardly, perhaps because her burqa was a bit loose. The attar shopkeeper rubbed a sample on the inside of her wrist. She smelled it intensely.

Out of nowhere, a group of men strolled through the street, blocking my view. Once they were gone, I could see the shop again.

Noor was not there.

I jumped up on my feet and ran in the direction of the shop. Hustling through another group of people, I felt my throat grow cold as I almost bumped against a man. I pushed him aside and stepped on the street. "Noor!" I shouted

"Noor!" I screamed, crossing to the other side. "Where are you, Noor?"

I approached the attar shop. "Where is the girl?" I howled at the shopkeeper.

He looked at me with baffled eyes and shrugged. He upturned his lower lip, gesturing he had no idea.

"She was here only a moment back," he looked around. "And then she disappeared."

"Don't lie," I shouted. "Where are you, Noor?"

My heart pounded out of control. All the possibilities ran in my head like a reel of nightmares. If I lost Noor at this juncture, my whole life would be ruined.

"Noor! Show up."

I was reaching for the collar of the shopkeeper when Noor emerged from behind the shop. She came running to me. I clutched her elbow tightly.

"Where did you go?"

"Awwh," she squealed in pain. "Awhhh!"

"Where were you?"

"I was – oh, leave me – the money flew out of my hand. A wind came, and, and I went after it. It flew over there – stop –"

I let go of her and went down on my knees before her. I looked at her face, which was on the verge of tears. So red, so soft.

"I am sorry," I said, inhaling long breaths, "I am sorry. I was worried for you." I ran a finger along the curve of her nose. "Come, tell me which bottle you want."

After purchasing three vials of attar, we walked towards my Toyota Fortuner. Although my nerves had calmed down somewhat, I could still feel my pulse throbbing at the base of my neck. Holding my hand, she swung my arm back and forth.

"Noor?" I said.

"Hmm?"

"I heard that your Arabic teacher came home yesterday."

"Hmm."

"What did he teach you?"

"He gave me two books. He said that there is no time to learn the letters. So I have to repeat what he says and keep it inside." She tapped her head.

"Did you learn anything?" I asked as I started the car.

Stuttering, she began to chant a single line that she said was from the Koran. She produced Parle-G biscuits from her burqa and tossed them out through the car's window at stray dogs. She repeated the same line, again and again, all the way back to my bungalow. Her recitation was in Arabic, rhythmic and singsong.

I did not bother asking her what it meant.

Chapter 9

Riju

Hearing footsteps behind us, Aziza and I turned around. It was Deenu. His eyes seemed scared, hands clasped together.

"There is a fight going on," he said, tilting his head towards the outer gate.

"What fight?" asked Aziza.

"I am not sure," Deenu said. "I heard that a girl is missing from Basirhat and people are furious about it." A scream came from down below. Deenu rushed to the railings. "We must leave now."

"But why are they here?" I asked, looking down. The man with the cleaver had entered the outer gate. He was brandishing his weapon in the air and shouting at the watchman. "Let us pass," he growled, "Or else, or else..." He swung the cleaver. It missed the arm of the watchman, who sat down crying.

Deenu tugged at my elbow. "He is blind with anger," he said. "It is Akhtar; I know him. He is mad. Let's go, now. Aziza *behen*, *dadaji* is waiting for you at the backdoor of the kitchen."

More yells came from below, *"Saalo ki itni jurrat!"* *"Betiyon ko uthate hai. Kutte. Tere ghar me bhi betiyaan hain yaad rakhna, saale namard kahinke."* "Today, I will finish whoever is inside. I will kill everyone." "*Kaat iss saale ko.* Cut him into pieces."

"The gatekeeper," Aziza's concerned voice reached my ears. "We must save him."

"Is the front door bolted?" I asked Deenu.

"I locked it from the inside."

The front door was thick and heavy, I remembered, with solid bolts. I counted on Akhtar and his friends having only sticks and a cleaver – not the best tools for breaking open a mammoth door. I wished that the men would not have the immediate sense to cover the back door. However, I was taking a considerable risk.

"Watchman," I shouted from the roof, "move away. Run."

The men looked up at me. They pushed the gatekeeper away and, in wild haste, ran towards the door.

We left the roof. We were hurrying down the stairs when the stone came. It crashed inside through the window, shattering the glass, and missed us. One of the shards, however, flew towards Aziza. She tried to duck but was too late. Next instant, she clutched the side of her neck with a painful cry. As she drew her hand away, blood coated the tip of her fingers.

We stopped. Deenu inspected her wound. The gash was deep, and it was clear that she would need stitches.

"The hospital is right next to the main bazaar," Deenu sounded panicked as he spoke. "We must take her there."

When we reached the ground floor, I heard fists pounding on the main door and voices thundering with rage. "Open the door! Open the door!"

"How far is the police station?" I asked Deenu while he directed us inside the kitchen behind the stairs. Aziza was out of sight.

"Two and a half kilometres from here," Deenu answered.

Loud cracking noise came from the door. I was wrong. The attackers had more weapons, which they now used in their attempt to loosen the bolts. If they broke in, I would have no choice but to fight them barehanded. Fending off six men untrained in combat would not be difficult, but I did not intend to get into a brawl at this moment.

"Where is Aziza?" I raised my voice, but I was calm. I was used to thinking straight in unpredictable situations.

Aziza emerged from the drawing hall and joined us in the kitchen. So I was not the only one with a cool head. Aziza had gone back to get a lock, which she hung on the kitchen door behind us.

Her cut was bleeding rather profusely now. She wrapped her dupatta around her neck. Although she tried to hide signs of pain, her twisted lips betrayed her.

Aziza's grandfather, a silver-haired man who walked with a straight spine even at seventy, waited for us at the backdoor.

"What happened *beti*?" he asked, shuddering at Aziza's wound.

"We are going to the hospital," I replied. I asked Deenu to reach the police station at once and tell them about what happened here.

While Deenu cycled off, Aziza, her grandfather and I got into the car of Aziza's grandfather. We rode in the direction of the hospital.

"Don't worry," Aziza said, gasping from the back seat. "I will be okay. A few stitches and-"

"No talking, please," I said. "Just lean back and try to relax."

Outside, the darkness falling over the earth seemed deeper than other days. Something abnormal was going on.

Human shadows moved about on the roads suspiciously. They were everywhere – in the gaps between the houses, behind lines of trees and fences, almost fading against the background of dark walls. They seemed more solid than ghosts, yet more secretive than people with harmless intentions. A few of them had canes in their hands, while the others had tools. Sickles and hovels, knives and hatchets, and even ladles. These men did nothing, just lurked. Six shadows talked among themselves next to the post office, their voices silent as the darkness.

Near the edge of the market, some of them were coming together, forming a group. They looked at our car as we passed by. One of them pointed at us, raised his arm, and said something. The others shook their heads and pushed his arm down. They went back into a shop that should not have been open at this hour of the day. Perhaps they decided that the time was not ripe, that their plans were not yet crystallized enough to be converted into actions.

Aziza and I noticed the smoke even before we had crossed the market. It rose from the same direction in which we were headed. The signboard that pointed to the hospital was lying by the road, its edges charred. A minute later, the flames came into view. Fire billowed out through a window of the hospital. Golden tongues licked at a car standing outside its gate. Smoke leaked out from the open front door and climbed along the wall. We did not see any patient or doctor. Most probably, all of them had fled.

"*Ya Allah,*" Aziza's grandfather gasped from the driver's seat.

"Turn the car around," I told him, "at normal speed."

Two shadow-like men emerged from behind the parking lot, from where more smoke swelled. They were carrying what looked like petrol cans in their hands. They stood still and watched us as our vehicle moved away.

"Keep driving," I said, "at normal speed."

None of us spoke till we had left the market behind us.

"Should we take her to Basirhat?" Aziza's grandfather asked.

"No," I said. "It is more than twenty-five kilometres away. There is another hospital by the western bank of the river. Let's go there."

As we drove ahead, only one thought surfaced in my head:

Something dangerous had begun, and it was spreading like lava from the mouth of a volcano.

Chapter 10

Vikram

Noor was fond of feeding street animals. She accumulated pieces of cakes, slices of bread and fruits from her food in a packet. On the rare occasions when I permitted her to step out, the girl looked out for a limping dog or a blind cat. If she spotted one, she let the creature gorge on her stockpile. It was an opportunity to set things right between Shiva and her, which was critical.

As the hours went by, the girl missed her mother increasingly, growing desperate to return home.

"*Bachhi*," I told her in the morning, "you must eat. Don't skip breakfast."

"Why did Shiva uncle bring me here?" Noor said with moist eyes.

"He will make it up to you."

She shook her head. "No, no. I want to go home, please."

"Soon, *bachhi*, soon."

"No!" she screamed, exploding, pushing the plate of food away. "Now!"

"Your *ammi* knows that you are here," I said assuringly. "Don't worry. She wants you home as soon as you can recite three paragraphs from the Koran. She said she will be really proud of you."

"*Ammi-hee-hee*," she cried.

"Uncle Shiva would like to say sorry by taking you on a trip."

"A trip?" she wiped her eyes. "Where?"

"The Elephanta caves."

"What is that?"

"You will see."

"I don't feel like going." She turned her face away, wiping tears off her face.

"We will ride a ferry and a toy train, a *chuk-chuk gaari*." I touched her. My fingers felt the young, tensed muscles running from her neck to shoulder. "However, I know what you will love more than anything else."

She looked at me, blinking away more tears.

"But I will not reveal it now," I said. "Dress up. Let's go."

I exited her room. Shiva was standing outside.

"This is your chance," I whispered to him. "Gain her trust. You know what to do."

On the way to the Elephanta caves from the Gateway of India, Noor, Shiva and I occupied a bench on the ferry. The sun sparkled on blue water as though laying down golden threads in crisscross patterns. I bought packets of chips and biscuits from the tiny shop inside the ferry, then passed them to Shiva.

"There," Noor leapt up in excitement, a finger pointing towards the sky. "There they are."

"Careful," I warned her, "don't lean over the edge."

The anticipated guests arrived in a large flock – the brown-headed gulls. They flew in closer to the ferry, legs tucked under white bodies, eyes surveying for food. Shiva tore open a packet of biscuits.

"Break it and toss it in the air," he told Noor.

"*Subhaan Allah*," she squealed in delight, crushing a biscuit. "They look like white dolphins with wings."

I watched on as Shiva and Noor kept flinging portions of biscuits at the gulls. The birds swooped in or dove down or shot upwards for catching the food mid-air. On most occasions, they succeeded, but a few times, the morsels slipped through their beaks, landing on the water. The fallen ones were scooped up by a gull that lagged behind. Soon other tourists on the boat joined in, aiming popcorns and other snacks at the hungry birds.

Noor clapped and jumped up in her seat. Propelled by thrill and eagerness, she clutched Shiva's hands whenever a gull flew too close to her.

"Give me more, Shiva uncle. More, more, more." She threw the birds flying kisses, spreading her arms like their majestic wings. In a moment of ecstasy, she burst into laughter and hugged Shiva. It appeared as though all the animosity she had for him melted away that moment.

I felt relieved. The plan was working. Shiva and Noor needed to bond, for I wanted to release the first video soon.

"Now, don't throw this biscuit," Shiva instructed her. "Hold it out between your fingers, like so. Let them come and get it."

Noor waited and waited, her outstretched arm offering chips. But this time, the birds showed no interest. They restricted themselves to seizing only the crumbs that came flying at them.

They won't come, I told myself. Unlike humans, they knew from birth the perils of trusting too much. They loved their freedom more than food.

I turned my attention to the rippling water. My memory leapt back across the years; I recalled the terrible waters I had experienced earlier in life. It had been the storm during which I had lost my true mother and had found a new one.

I was born to a low-caste family in Bhubaneswar. In 1971, when I was seven, my parents and I were visiting a relative in Paradeep. On the second day of our stay, the weather department issued warnings of a cyclone that would later go down in history as the destroyer of numerous lives.

We had thought that we were far away from the eye of the cyclone. But we were wrong. We became scared when the wind began to blow fiercely, shooting sand inside our hotel room. We could see the beach far away through the window. The wind was ferociously quick in picking up pace, its invisible arms uprooting coconut trees with ease. Its wildness covered the sky with flying rubbles and dust.

That day I learnt that the thing closest to God was nature.

My mother, my first mother, wrapped her arms tightly around me. She broke into a wail. My eyes stayed on the window as the mayhem rumbled closer and closer. It picked up cows on its way and threw them away. It felt as though the whole earth had gone off its axis, spinning madly. The howls of the storm became so loud that I could no longer hear the cries of my mother.

Then it hit us. It crashed into our hotel with titanic force and massacred everything. Our family was scattered. I hid under the bed with no idea where others were blown away.

The rains followed a short time later, grey in colour, torrential in might. I remembered the following events in torn memories that I could never remove from my head, no matter how much I tried. The rain blinded us. The roof of our hotel was flung away. Next, the walls gave in, and water flooded our room, sweeping me away. Soon everything around me became black.

When I opened my eyes, I found myself lying on a beach. Before I could make sense of anything, more than ten women were pulling at my arms and legs. They snapped at each other. They cried, their faces twisted by shock and fear.

"Leave him," a woman wailed, "he is my kid!"

"Son, my son, my son!" another woman screamed.

"Please, he is the only one I have left," a third voice came.

"I will call the police if you don't let him go."

"Stop hurting him. You are killing my child!"

"It's a boy! Give him to me."

"Oh God, how will I live now. Aw-ha-ha."

None of them was my mother. None of them asked me who my mother was.

After fighting for a long while, the women began to go away one by one. They looked for other children half-buried in the sand – nameless infants they could claim as their own. Boys featured higher than girls in their wishlist. Amidst all the commotion, a girl sat naked on the ground with tears on her face. She was wounded, and she cried for help. But no one picked her up.

Finally, a woman succeeded in wresting me away from the others. She wiped me with her pallu and observed my features. She would turn out to be my new mother, Rukmini Rathore.

Her husband, Mr Rathore, was a respectable civil servant. He was rather indifferent with the whole affair. He faced no problem in arranging my birth certificate. Then, my new mother passed away from kidney failure. Once she was gone, *pitaji* grew warm towards me, as though he had been unsure of showing his true feelings when his wife had been around. He educated me. I followed his footsteps into the Indian Administrative Service.

No one in my new family ever questioned where I came from. I never mentioned my past; I was loved even more because of this. My journey from a lowly belonging to an influential family helped me in one particular aspect: It made me hungry for power. And so, I kept on rising through the ranks in the ladder of bureaucracy.

Then, *pitaji* was killed some years later, and my life retook a new turn.

I realized much later that the cyclone had taught me two important lessons, although I had been too young to understand them back then.

First, we had at least partial control over our fates. Mrs Rathore did not give up. She fought for me and won me. She brought me into her family, changing the course of events forever.

Second, a wounded girl without clothes was like a Goddess fallen from grace, a ruined flower. It was people's nature to recoil in horror on seeing her.

Now, back on the ferryboat, my phone rang, breaking off the thread of thoughts. Seeing a familiar number on display, I walked away from Noor and Shiva.

"Yes," I said into the phone.

"Sahib," a voice spoke from the other side, "I was saying that I have news."

I held my breath. "Go on."

"It has started," he said. "The Muslims began by burning the hospital near the market. It was owned by a Hindu."

Immediately, a wave of relief washed over me. However, it died soon as I reminded myself that this was only the first stage.

"Is it moving in the expected direction?" I asked.

"Yes," the voice replied. "I talked to several people out there. They are seething with hatred. It is only a matter of time before they explode. That is what I was saying."

"Ah, good," I said, expressing satisfaction even though I knew that the information was most probably exaggerated. People's imaginations ran ahead of actual events, especially when they tried to appease their masters.

"What now?" he asked.

"Don't let it fizzle away," I said. "Make it grow bigger. The faster, the better. The more violent, the better."

"Hmm. Sahib, I was saying that, what about my payment?"

"Also," I said, "I will share something with you today evening. Spread it to all the news channels."

"Ji, Sahib," he said.

"Keep texting me the details."

"Ji, Sahib," he said. "And my payment?"

"You will get it before due time. Don't worry."

I cut the call. My eyes painted the scenery before me with happiness. The grey navy ships shone in broad daylight while the sea-marker poles danced on the water with more vigour. A determined cargo ship swayed by gracefully. The gulls carried the colour of the sky in their eyes.

But I stopped myself from getting overjoyed with initial success. Even after accomplishing everything, I knew there would be a need for more. No country ever ran out of work to be done.

When hatred found a reason to express itself in the form of violence, riots took birth. The Muslims of Basirhat had always lived with suppressed animosity. Noor's kidnapping merely acted as a flicker of fire in the gunpowder. They are using the abduction as an excuse to burn and kill – how dare the Hindus?

Now the cycle of revenge would take over, moving to and fro between religions. And soon, the rage of the Muslims would turn into self-destruction.

I, however, would take nothing for granted. I needed to keep reminding the Muslims why they started the fight. Then I would give them a final push so that they fell over the edge.

I looked at Noor. I again thought about the softness of her skin. It sent shivers down my fingers. My intention was clear: I wanted to destroy her.

I could picture what would happen after I was done with the girl. To her, death would seem friendlier than life. Her tormented innocence would make her rush into the bathroom repeatedly, trying to wash away the sin from her skin. But the sin lived somewhere else, in someone else's heart. Her brain would not let her body sleep, and her plundered body would not allow her brain to forget.

She would be forever suspicious of men. She would think that she could never be free because she was a girl. Everywhere, every second of the day, she would feel conscious of her vulnerability. It would stretch beyond her life, her generation, and never end.

Alas, she would never comprehend that her sacrifice served a far greater cause.

Radical thoughts, I reminded myself, must be naked, without subtleties. So here was my intention, simply put:

I will rape the Muslim girl.

This Goddess must fall from grace. It was unfair but necessary.

Chapter 11

Riju

We entered the Emergency room of the Government Hospital in Basirhat. We did not have to wait for long before the doctor arrived.

"I am Dr Batra," he said jovially, "and I am not a hair specialist." He arched backwards and began a burst of laughter that went away when he saw that we were not amused.

The doctor, bustling with energy, inspected Aziza's injured neck. "You can relax," he declared. "There is no glass fragment in your wound, and the cut did not sever any major blood vessel. However, the injury is deep. You will need stitches. Come with me."

He took Aziza behind the curtains as her grandfather stared after them with a worried face.

"She will be okay," I ventured to calm him down. "Some doctors feel they must lift up the spirits of theirs patients."

He took a seat and kept rubbing his lips with the back of his hand. I sat down beside him.

"What is all this, Riju?" he asked. "Who were those people who tried to attack us?"

"I have no-"

"Look," he interrupted, drawing my attention to a man sitting in front. He was playing a news channel on his mobile phone. He wore earphones, so we could not hear what he was listening to. But on the top margin of the screen was written, "Kidnapped Basirhat girl's video released."

I pulled out my phone and started the news. "...according to the police," the newsreader spoke, "Noor's mother has confirmed that the girl in the video is her daughter. This video was posted on YouTube less than an hour back, and you are watching it exclusively on The News Forum. Is the man in the clip her kidnapper? Is this where Noor is kept hostage? The police are trying to find answers to these questions. They are also tracking the device from which this sensational footage was uploaded. Here is another look at the video:"

The news anchor disappeared, and the image of a girl surfaced. She was about six or seven years old. She wore a burqa with golden designs on the sleeves and the neckline. Although a piece of cloth hung behind her to hide the background, the bluish surrounding suggested that she was in a room lit by tube light. She looked confused, unaware of the camera filming her from one corner. She held a book in her hand, which she flipped this way and that. It was the Koran.

The next moment a man appeared and took his place before her. He had a bulky figure with bulging love handles. His face was covered with a clown mask. Seeing him, the girl laughed.

"How am I looking, *gudia*?" the man asked.

The girl managed between shakes of laughter, "Joker, joker, *'pling'* uncle is a joker."

The *'pling'* was used to hide the name of the man.

"And who is this?" The man produced a teddy bear from his back.

"Baadshah," the girl pointed at the toy.

"And who is Baadshah's best friend?" he asked.

"Me, me, and only me."

"Me who? Tell me your name, *gudia.*"

"You know my name."

"I do, but," the man pointed at the red nose of the mask, "joker uncle does not know."

"Oh right," the girl said and widened her eyes as though playing along. "Hello, joker uncle, I am Noor."

"Hi, Noor," the man said. "You look lovely. And you smell fantastic. Is that attar?"

Noor nodded.

"Wow," he gestured at the book. "What were you reading?"

"This, I was reading the Koran."

"The Koran? What is that?"

"It is the holy book," she said, her lips drawing a big pout while uttering 'holy book'. "It has the words of Allah."

"Dear God, you know a lot, Noor. Excellent. Here is your prize." He handed the teddy to her. "And I have another gift for you."

The girl kept the Koran aside, sat the bear on her lap, and extended her arms.

"Give it to me," she said.

"You can't take it in your hands," the man said, laughing, "You have to take it on your cheek."

Noor looked puzzled. Before she could react, the man grabbed her chin and planted a hard kiss on her cheek, rubbing the lips of his mask against her skin. Noor squealed, shocked by the sudden attack. The man leant back and sniggered as she squirmed and wiped her face vigorously. She began shedding muffled tears.

"Did you like that, Noor?"

Noor stayed silent, curling into herself and looking away.

The clown-man laughed for a while, then lapsed into seriousness. "Don't cry. Stop, please. See what I have here – a camera. Yes, come here, look. *Ammi* can see you."

Noor turned at the screen. Quickly wiping her moist eyes with her sleeves, she jumped up.

"*Ammi!*" she shouted and waved both hands over her head as if forgetting all about the kiss a minute back, "*ammi, ammi, ammijaan!*"

"That's enough," the clown-man said. "Now we have to leave. Tell your mom that you are doing fine here."

Noor gave him a hesitant head shake and repeated something censored by an edited noise. The man replied in a murmur drowned by a digital sound. At the end of it, Noor turned again at the camera.

"*Ammi*," she said through teeth set tight from reluctance, "*ammi*, I am alright. I will come home soon."

The recording ended. The newsreader returned.

"The investigators are analyzing this disturbing video for clues," she said. "According to our special sources, the police is not yet sure about what the kidnapper wants. He has not demanded any ransom, making one think if a second tape is coming next. On the other hand, Heena Mustafa, Noor's mother, verified that this attire does not belong to her daughter. The expensive Hamley's teddy bear and the golden embroidered burqa raises speculations about whether her kidnapper is affluent. However, the ACP Dhritiman Banerjee has refused to comment on the clip. Meanwhile, there have been reports of violence in and around Basirhat, the hometown of Noor. More on it after this break."

"So this is why the people of Basirhat are furious," Aziza's grandfather said.

I said nothing. I was drowned in thoughts.

"Did you notice his locket?" he asked me.

"Yes," I said as the image of the clown-man flashed in my mind. A locket of Lord Shiva had dangled from his necklace.

"It was hardly visible," Aziza's grandfather said, "but I noticed it."

"It was visible nonetheless," I said.

"Maybe it can be a clue for the police."

"No, grandpa, it was a statement to reveal that a Hindu has taken away a Muslim girl."

He shook his head, muttering, "*Ya Allah.*"

"And I am sure the police knows that the abductor wants religious violence. They are not publicizing it because that would make matters worse."

We fell silent till Dr Batra came back with Aziza and presented her with a flourish of his hands.

"She is a strong lady," the doctor announced. "She did not whimper at all."

Aziza, who had a white bandage stuck to the side of her neck, gave a weak smile.

"Take these medicines," Dr Batra said, pointing at a prescription. "It is normal if she feels weak for a while, but she must not go hungry. The stitches will stay for a week." He enthusiastically called out for the next patient as we came out of the room.

Heading for Basirhat, in the car, I told Aziza about the video. She listened without a word, staring at the road.

We stopped at a petrol pump. Not too far away, a cowherd was walking by with his livestock. A group of men came out from behind a bush and stood blocking his path. Sickles, shovels and pickaxes glistened in their hands. An argument ensued. The leader of the group snatched off the skullcap of the cowherd. Then he started to drag away one of the cows, which refused to go with him. The poor cowherd fell down on his knees and pleaded with folded hands. Setting the cow loose, the leader gripped its owner's hand and hauled him along the ground.

I couldn't stay quiet any longer. I got off the car. I was about to raise my voice when a man rushed out from the petrol pump.

"Have you gone mad?" he screamed at the leader, "let him go right now."

"Go back inside," the leader growled, not loosening his grip, "One of these Muslims beat up my brother this morning. And look at this *madarchod.*" He kicked the cowherd in his ribs. "He has tied *tabeez* around the necks of the cows. *Saale gaumata ko Musalmaan banayega!*"

"I said, release him."

"This is none of your business. Do you want us to burn your little petrol pump?"

"If you don't leave him alone," the petrol pump man said, "I won't teach Piku for free anymore."

That made the leader stop in his tracks. He spat slang at the cowherd. Shoving him away, he retreated with his fellowmen, muttering, "*Chalo, chalo.*"

Our car seemed like a block of shame, disgust, and concern back on the road. How could humanity stoop so low? Even those cows appeared better behaved than the humans surrounding them.

"Vigilantism is the new name of revenge," Aziza's grandfather said. "It's so unfortunate."

"Grandpa, complaining is not going to help," Aziza stirred up. "This is criminal behaviour."

"Can't we do something about it?" her grandfather asked.

I said nothing till we dropped the old man at his house and assured him we would return in a short while.

"I see a starting point," I said from the driver's seat, "but I can't, at any cost, let my name get involved. It will ruin-"

"Don't worry," Aziza interrupted. "I will take every responsibility. What do you have in mind?"

"We have to find the girl," I said. "Her disappearance is the root of all problems."

"You are right," she agreed. "But we don't have any clue of her whereabouts."

I considered for a moment how safe it would be to let her in on another secret. I was under the impression that no one in this country was as selfless as the army and the police. Moreover, politics had built such a dirty image for itself. It seemed impossible for a politician to take dangers head-on. I thought politicians were good actors and reactors but bad at being proactive. However, the injured Aziza, glowing with bravery, was eager to stop a calamity that had already begun.

Trusting her might not be harmful.

"Dhritiman Banerjee," I said, "the Inspector in charge of Noor's case belonged to the same IPS cadre as me. We last talked more than six months back, although he does not know what I actually do."

I called up Dhritiman from my mobile but got a busy tone. After a few minutes, he rang me back.

"Arrey yaar," he said, "where have you been?"

"I was a bit busy with work," I said. "What is up with you nowadays? Big man, huh, handling big cases."

He laughed in his signature nasal tone. "At least I did not vanish like you. The other day I was talking to Aakash. He said that you are the camphor man. Because of the way you vanished, you see."

"I could not help it," I said. "I was sent to a rural posting, because of which my phone didn't detect any signal."

"I understand, yaar. I have also been quite busy lately. This kidnapping case that I am handling is all over the news. You must have heard about it."

"I saw it in the news."

"I see, I see. So that's how you remembered me."

"I have wanted to call for a while now." I felt guilty for not being in touch. "But tell me more about it."

"Arrey yaar, it's a strange affair. Listen to this. A CCTV camera in Howrah station caught the girl, Noor, climbing into the Mumbai bound weekly express train. Inside the train, she was sitting with a short man. But the man disappeared from the train the next afternoon. Since then, Noor had been sitting alone."

"Where did she go from there?" I turned the car into an unfamiliar alley and parked it in a corner. I did not want to run into another huddle of vengeful shadows.

"Exactly," Dhritiman said. "Now comes the most curious part. Around eleven at night, the train stopped at a station. After that, no one saw Noor. When I enquired if anyone saw her leave the train I got three answers. Some said it was too dark to see since the lights were out. According to a few, a man carried the girl through the corridor, sleeping in his arms. The rest said that a woman, not a man, took her away."

"Someone must be lying," I said.

"Hold on, there's more strangeness. The witnesses who saw Noor with a man sat on the left side in the coach. However, the people who spotted her with a woman were on the opposite side. I mean, what kind of a riddle is this, yaar?"

"Wasn't this the man who sat with Noor before?"

"No. This person was bulky."

"So you have two groups of witnesses present in the same compartment, looking at the same event and telling two different stories?"

"Yes," he said. "Because of this peculiar situation, we have no idea how to go ahead. We are examining more CCTV footage from all the stoppages. But it has been a futile exercise till now."

"Then there's a high possibility that the cameras missed them altogether," I said.

"In addition," he said, "this kidnapping has begun a fit of religious violence in Basirhat."

"That is where I am right now," I revealed. He deserved to know at least this bit of truth. It was safe, and it would help ease my guilt for feeding him multiple lies. "I came here for spending my holidays."

"Oh no. Get out of there immediately. The situation might very well escalate to a full-fledged riot. Already several buildings have been torched."

"Relax. I will be alright."

"I am serious, yaar. Leave right away. Okay, tell me your exact location. I will dispatch a unit to fetch you."

"Alright, alright. See, I am even ignoring the fact that you are asking an IPS officer to run away from danger."

"You don't understand," he sounded frustrated. "Basirhat is a hotspot of religious violence and cross-border smuggling. You have no inkling about all the forces at work there. The situation is complicated."

"Fine, I will start for Kolkata at once."

"Yes, be safe. Listen, I am getting another call now. There's a lot of pressure from the superiors to solve this case quickly. I will catch up with you again when I am not in a hurry."

After returning the phone to my pocket, I filled in Aziza on the conversation. She kept fading into phases of deep thoughts over and over as I drove towards her grandfather's house. We decided that we would pick him up and leave for Kolkata. She had some relatives and friends there to spend a few days.

I dialled my home number. I asked my elder brother to take his wife away from Basirhat until the unrest subsided. Soon afterwards, Dhritiman's name came up on my phone's screen.

"Hello?" He sounded excited.

"What's the matter?" I asked.

"We have a breakthrough. The video surveillance team informed me that the station's CCTV captured a glimpse of Noor near the main exit."

"Great news. Who accompanied her?"

"That, unfortunately, wasn't visible. The station was packed with people."

"Wait," I said, "hold on. Which station are you talking about?"

"Arrey yaar, I forgot to mention it. Dadar Central. She seemed to be sleeping on the shoulder of whoever took her."

"Sleeping or unconscious," I said, then paused for a moment, thinking. "If Noor was near the exit, there is little chance she boarded another train from there. Oh, this is becoming more complicated. Mumbai is the capital of human trafficking in India; numerous places to hide a girl."

"I know," he said. "Mumbai police and we will jointly work on this case. I am updating you because you sounded interested in it. Now I must rush into a meeting on whether we should make this information public. Quickly, what's your opinion?"

I took a pause, running the pros and cons in my head. "Let's hold it back for now."

"But the heat in Basirhat might simmer down if everyone knows that we have made some inroads in the matter."

"I understand. However, we must not alert the criminal."

"But the people of Basirhat might see the logic of-"

"Dhritiman," I stopped him, "when men engage in revenge, they become blind to logic."

I heard his sharp breaths against the phone.

"Fine yaar," he said, "let me hear what others in my team have to say. After all, how much harm can a little bit of delay cause, right?"

I did not miss his nervous tone. Both of us knew, in this situation, how much difference every minute of living with a wrong decision could make.

"Un-huh," I answered. "If I have any theories on how Noor was taken, I will inform you."

I put the phone aside and turned to Aziza.

"Mumbai," I said to her. "Noor has been spotted in Mumbai."

A look of fright and concern made a brief appearance on her face before her jaws clenched in determination. We reached her grandfather's house, our arrival coinciding with the withdrawal of the last sunrays. She told him that she needed to leave for Mumbai immediately. I had expected shadows of curiosity in the eyes of the old man. But instead, he calmly suggested that we take the car to the Dum Dum airport. He would ride the bus to Kolkata and stay with a relative.

As Aziza went inside the house to get her luggage, her grandfather pulled me aside. "I have spent decades fighting for power," he said. "I know everything about identity politics. So take my word on this. No matter what you think, keep no doubt that Aziza would have done nothing less had Noor been a Hindu girl."

I would have loved to trust his words. I admired Aziza's actions. Her concern for the girl seemed sans any impurity. But my job and experience taught me that judging someone from actions alone could result in grave mistakes.

Aziza and I drove towards the Dum Dum airport without knowing where to go once we reached Mumbai.

Chapter 12

Vikram

The news anchor before me was dressed in clothes of self-importance. The tips of his shoes shone under the studio lights. He wore a red tie and a black blazer. He had a square face, and his lips almost stretched from ear to ear in a grin. He was an English-channel journalist who perhaps thought he was the best at his job because he spoke in a neutral accent.

This was media, the necessary circus of India.

I kept my back upright. My fingertips were joined together, showing approachability. I had clean-shaved an hour ago, which made me look more reliable.

"Vikram Rathore," he started, "ex-IAS, ex-governor of Assam, the man with numerous great feats to his name, welcome. So please tell us, what exactly is Dilon Main Mohabbat?"

"It is my retirement plan," I said with a chuckle. "Seriously, however, Dilon Main Mohabbat was formed in 2008 to bring back the lost ambience of peace in areas hit by violence. The Prime Minister of India wanted a trustworthy leader at its helm. I was honoured to accept his offer."

"And why did you take it?"

"Because I thought I had not done enough for this country, for its brilliant people. I wanted to do more. I believe that by calming people down in an agitated area, I am saving the country."

"You mean you are saving the citizens' lives?" he asked.

"Not just saving lives," I replied. "When hate-violence takes place, it affects the mentalities of everyone. Children can't play together, people don't talk to each other, and no one trusts the administration. The foundation of a happy society breaks down. And the worst part is, it does not stop. The hostility gets passed on to future generations."

"But don't you think everyone is strong enough to realize it themselves?"

"They are," I nodded. "However, sometimes people are blinded by anger. They panic. It's basic human nature. We try to help them come out of the horrible situation."

"There have been instances, Rathoreji, where people have said that they don't need any help. I'm talking about what happened in Patna last year. People said that you were interfering in their personal matters."

"What might be personal for some is national for us. See, wherever we go, we find a few men who want to cause trouble. So, even if the citizens feel they can handle the situation, they are often not capable enough. We make them understand the importance of peace."

"Don't you think it's the police's duty?"

"It's the duty of everyone," I said. "And besides, when people become angry, they lose faith in the police. In such cases, it really helps if someone shows them the path. Someone without a uniform."

"And how do you guide them?"

"We talk to them, trying to understand their concerns. We help them think straight when emotions tend to take over. But-" I paused.

"But?" he asked me.

"But understanding their problems is the beginning," I said. "We take their issues to the concerned authorities. Then we sit with them to plan out a solution. We even take part in implementing the necessary steps."

"It is curious," he leant back. "From being the representative of the government, you turn into representatives of the people."

"We represent everyone. The government and the people always co-exist. We act as the bridge between them. See, although I was appointed by the Prime Minister, my position demands me to stay unbiased."

"So, after so many years into it, would you say that you have remained unbiased all along?"

A flash of memory came to me – my father lying on the floor, in a dim corner, chanting:

"Jaatasya hi dhruvo mrityur dhruvam janma mritasya cha; tasmad apariharye arthe na tvam shochitum arhasi." (Death is certain of that which is born. Birth is

certain of that which is dead. Therefore, one should not mourn over the inevitable.)

With every word came out a trickle of blood from the wound of his belly, and I wiped it with a bare hand. He tried to look at me but could not open his eyes because of the unbearable pain.

"*Pitaji*," I said, sobbing, glancing at the knife stabbed into his navel, "should I pull it out?"

"*Jaatasya hi dhruvo mrityur dhruvam janma mritasya cha...*" he repeated, shaking his head slowly. I watched him, not crying for help because *they* would know that I was alive.

Since that day, it had been impossible to stay unbiased.

The reporter cleared his throat now. "Have you been successful in being unbiased, Rathoreji?"

"Yes," I said.

"But then, unbiasedness does not guarantee success, does it?"

"I did not get you."

"I am talking about Srinagar," he said.

I stopped myself from placing one knee on top of another, crossing my arms, and going into a closed posture.

"And it wasn't the only occasion where your team failed," he added. "This happened in Chennai last year: A cow belonging to a temple entered a mosque, or, allegedly, someone pushed it into a mosque. The killings that followed-"

"I remember the case."

"You went there after three months. Three months. And you could not host a gathering because of public protest. It resulted in more violence."

"First of all, Dilon main Mohabbat is not the Rapid Action Force. It waits for the law to take its course because that is necessary. We enter the scene afterwards to sew the torn threads of social and psychological bonding."

"But in Chepauk-"

"Yes, coming back to that," I said. "Either your research is incomplete, or you deliberately allowed me to highlight our persistence. If it's the latter, thank you. We went to Chennai a second time. And our visit ended up being much more successful than our initial efforts. So, you see, we don't give up. But we realize that we have begun a mission that will never get completed. It is an ongoing process. Religious harmony is not a destination; it is a way of life."

Although the anchor's eyes seemed to have lost a bit of enthusiasm, his smile was unbreakable. He nodded, consulted his notes before looking back up.

"Azad Khan," he said, "in a press conference last month, said that you are the finest orator of this country."

"I thank him for his compliment. I, although, feel that a lot remains to be done. Perhaps Azad likes me because he is an old friend."

"So, Azad, the President of the Nagrik Ekta Dal and a renowned politician, mentioned your name in his party's national conference. Does that mean something?"

"I am not interested in joining politics," I said, "if that is what you are asking."

"If not politics, what next?"

"Leading my team has given me a wonderful opportunity to serve our society. It is such a unique idea. Right now, I am not thinking about anything beyond it."

The journalist did not seem satisfied with my reply. He, like all newspersons, was looking for dirt. The truth was not his business; business was his only truth.

This was media, the necessary dung-beetle of India.

He encircled something in his notes, then said, "I know I'm raising the same point again, but I don't understand it. You were a part of the bureaucracy, but you felt the need to step out of the system and start a-"

"Sir," Shiva's voice cut in. He came running to me from behind the camera and handed me a piece of paper. I read it as the anchor looked on, baffled.

"Excuse me-" the reporter began.

"No," I interrupted, "excuse me. This interview must end now. I must leave."

"But we can't finish it like this. It will be abrupt."

"Hmm," I said, my heartbeats still recovering from the shock of what was written on the paper. "Alright. Edit out your last question and quickly ask for my final words."

"Okay," the interviewer said and looked at the director, who gave him a thumbs up. "Do you have any message for our audience?"

I had several versions of this answer ready in my head. I had one version for the villagers, one for the atheists, another for the middle class, and many more. Now, I chose the variant curated for the urban English-speaking audience.

"Yes," I said. "We must believe that everyone is innately good. And violence is not a normal act of human beings. Discrimination and classes exist everywhere – cities and villages alike. We must start intelligent discussions and charity and spread our love for each other. In the coming years, I want you to make Dilon Main Mohabbat redundant. *Bharat ki jai, bharatvaasion ki jai.*"

As I hurriedly walked out of the studio, I once again opened the piece of paper clutched in my hand. I read it once more:

The fun has begun.

***

I rushed back home and switched on the TV. The express news began, presenting quick summaries of all the important happenings.

Nowadays, the world is replete with popcorn versions of everything — sports, movies, politics, news. Over the years, as people's lifespan had expanded, their attention span had shrunk. They now preferred everything in quicker, shallower formats, looking for entertainment even in places where it did not exist.

As the TV showed how the violence unfolded in Basirhat and its adjoining areas, relief washed over me. More than four dozen vehicles were set on fire, allegedly by the Muslims. In reply, the Hindus assaulted everyone in a procession on the eve of Muharram. As a result, more than seventy injured people – their real blood mixed with the fake blood painted on their backs for the festival – were admitted to the Taaki Municipal Hospital. Amusingly enough, a group of Muslim men burnt down the hospital, not knowing their own people were undergoing treatment inside. Several men, women and children could not make it out alive.

In another part of the city, the moustache-less beards killed a family on their way to a temple. But later, the Hindus triumphed by impaling ten men in a local mosque with trishuls. Then the skull caps tried to settle the scores by looting four public buses. They left the buses standing on flaming tyres. Behind a slum, the police found a pile of several women in the bushes. The culprits had tortured the helpless before bashing in their heads, blurred in the image telecasted.

However, there had been no news of any violence for the last ten hours. The newsreader said that it was a sign that people were calming down. But I had enough experience in riots to know better. I knew that people on both sides must be making good use of this intermission by heaping arms and ammunition. They were getting ready for a more explosive outburst.

The pictures of damaged heads brought back old memories. On Tuesday, May 26, 1987, I was new in the Civil

Services. I had been running frantically towards my home in Meerut. It had been three days since the Provincial Armed Constabulary had supposedly massacred a small Muslim population in Maliana. The open killings gave momentum to the riot that had started a few days back.

While rushing, I accidentally kicked a crushed skull on the pavement. It made me stop short. I took a moment to compose myself, feeling sick. But I had to save *pitaji*, so I began running again. As I neared our house, which stood behind a mosque, the stench of burnt bodies choked my nostrils. I climbed the stairs to our apartment, jumping over rivulets of blood that rolled into the drain on the side.

I found the door wide open.

"*Pitaji!*" I called out. After a pause, I heard a painful grumble from somewhere inside.

As a cold weakness spread in the middle of my chest, I hurried inside. My eyes fell on the wall of our drawing-room, from where the TV had been uprooted. In black letters, someone had written,

"Agar nafrat tumhara dharm hai,

Toh inteqam humara Allah hai."

(If hatred is your religion,

Then revenge is our Lord.)

"*Pitaji!*" I screamed, the soles of my feet turning into ice. "Where are you?"

"Beta...aaa...," a voice whimpered.

In a bewildered state of mind, I flew to the bathroom. I found father lying down. Blood spread across the floor under him like a satanic halo. His chest bore stabbing marks while the handle of a knife rose from a gash on his stomach. I tore my eyes away from the entrails that were pushing out from his wound. I fell down on my knees, crying, and brought his head up on my lap. Although it was a miracle that he was still breathing, I knew that I was too late.

"Why...why did you come, beta?" father mumbled. "They will be...go away and..." His words failed to find a voice. He gave up.

I ran my fingers into his wet hair and looked at his eyes directed towards the ceiling. Then, without warning, he began to chant.

"*Jaatasya hi dhruvo mrityuh dhruvam janma mritasya cha; tasmaadaparihaarye arthe na tvam shochitumarhasi.*" (Death is certain of that which is born. Birth is certain of that which is dead. Therefore, you should not mourn over the inevitable.)

He chanted the shloka, again and again, his lips moving sluggishly. I wanted to pull out the knife from his body, but he said there was no need. Then, in a whisper, he summoned me closer to him.

"They...out there," he said. "They're out there. They will come back. Beta, you have to decide your religion for today."

He fell silent. His eyes were frozen on me. Holding his lifeless head in my arms, I exploded into a howl. Then, I became quiet.

Even though deep anguish and anger blinded my senses, I could clearly see the meaning of his last words. I pulled the knife out of his belly and went to the refrigerator. It was toppled sideways on the floor but still functioning. I took out the ice tray and went inside my bedroom, bolting the door. Shutting my eyes, I considered my choices. I could pretend to be one of them or die as a Hindu in this locality of Muslims, who were now overtaken by madness.

I decided that stubbornness was good, but only till it did not become foolishness.

I took off my clothes, still crying and trembling, and stood naked in front of the mirror. I stretched the foreskin of my penis, held it with my fingers. I placed the edge of the knife over my loose Hindu skin. I recalled the sacrifices that Krishna had told Arjun would be crucial for winning the battle of Kurukshetra. As I began to cut, I did not take my eyes off my reflection. Moving the knife from one side to another, I kept on deepening the cut.

I did not feel much pain, for grief had already filled my body. The sharp knife performed its duty, slicing through my foreskin. Once it was over, I dipped my converted penis into the ice tray and sat down in the corner of the room. My crotch, thighs and fingers lay covered in blood. I waited for the return of the Muslims. They would discover the audacity of a Hindu to mock their religion and kill me instantly.

But they did not come. I filled the tray with fresh ice cubes, waiting for my circumcision to heal. Outside, people used the cover of darkness to murder others and often did not know the religion of their victims. They ripped away clothes from the carcasses and raped women and men indiscriminately. Violence ran amok.

I heard screams every now and then outside the door. Voices calling out names. Screams. Footsteps coming near, wandering, then going away. Once, the clinks of metallic weapons reached my ears as a few men entered our house. They walked to the bathroom, noticed my father, and laughed. Then they left. *Pitaji*, even after his death, continued to protect me.

I avoided using the bathroom. I emptied my bladder in the corner of the bedroom, shutting my mouth against the piercing pain of urine against the open wound. I spent seven nights that saw shops and houses burn into flames and seven mornings that witnessed smokes and cries rising into the sky. Then, finally, wrapping a loincloth around my waist, I stepped outside.

But I did not get far. Four men in vests and chequered lungis, armed with swords, confronted me in an alleyway. One of them placed his weapon on the base of my neck and asked, "Whom do you offer your prayers, Allah or Ishwar?"

I discovered right there that, along with my foreskin, fear had left my body.

I held my head high. "Allah," I said.

The man nodded but did not take his eyes off me because my answer had failed to convince him. He lowered his sword and, with its tip, began to lift my loincloth. My stomach clenched.

"Aslam, police!" a man shouted as he came scampering from the far side of the alley. "Police. Run. Run."

The sword-wielding man and the rest of his group vanished. I hurried onto the main road and found that the informer was wrong – it was not the police but the army. I stopped one of their trucks and requested the driver to rescue me.

"Who are you?" the driver gave me a suspicious look.

"My name is Vikram Rathore," I said. "IAS 1985 batch, Delhi cadre."

His eyes widened at once, and his expression became alert. "We have come to round up the violent ones. Get in, please."

"Thank you. And there is something else I want to tell you."

He waited, raising his eyebrows.

"I saw four men running that way," I said. "They were armed. Let's catch them first."

If my natural birth happened when Rukmini Rathore picked me up from a beach, I found my purpose the day my father departed. It was simple: the Muslims had to be eliminated from this country. My rage for them intensified further during my days as a bureaucrat and later as a Governor. The *other* religion, I realized, was the source of all problems. They claimed demands on the food and water meant for us and made hostility a commonplace affair. The ungrateful bastards wanted equal treatment, even though they should have been satisfied that we allowed them to live in our land. They had taken our kindness for our weakness. Ideally, violence-mongers like them should not just be kicked out but also punished.

However, as long as I held a public position, I found it difficult to take steps towards causing them any harm. I was scared of getting exposed. So I had to wear the mask of fairness all the time. And I worked hard to keep the cover in place. My conscious efforts of pretending to support equality made me better at it than anyone else. My rapport of carrying out my duty impeccably well spread fast. I rose to success in no time, becoming the youngest Governor the country ever saw.

Although I was not interested in marriage, a wife always helped gain public trust. The ideal man, people thought, could balance his profession and family at the same time. Thus I tied the knot.

But my stint in the office was not a completely dry period. I ordered the demolition of Muslim slums, retracted permissions for building Islamic educational institutes, and considered religion a significant factor while promoting officers to higher ranks. But I acted with subtleness all the time, even though I loathed the delicate ways. Lucky for me, everyone mistook my partiality as sternness.

"Sir is very strict in protecting environmental laws. That is why no one can build anything near the beach, not even madrasas."

"Sir did the right thing by ordering the police to shift the mosque. The highway under construction could not go around it. Sir puts common interest above all, you see."

"We support Mr Vikram Rathore's banning of beef shops. Why butcher an animal considered sacred by someone else when other animals can be used to serve the purpose? He took this decision to prevent communal tension. Anyway, most of the shops that were shut down did not have a licence."

However, such changes presented themselves rarely, making me wait a long time. Besides, I realized that these small acts would never create a major impact. It was not enough – *pitaji* would whisper in my dreams. Pretty soon, the hatred growing inside me, unable to explode, began suffocating me. I was failing; failure made me mad. So, a few years ago, I took voluntary retirement because I needed time to think about what I should do next.

My thoughts were presently interrupted as the news began to repeat the video I released yesterday. I shot the clip to destroy the brief lull that had descended on Basirhat, reminding everyone about their anger. And it hit its mark. The Chief Minister of West Bengal, replaying her usual rant, condemned the kidnapping. But more importantly, a whole Hindu locality was demolished by unknown men.

At my home, too, the situation had become tense, but it was expected. Noor had gone into a shell of silence and had refused to break it since last night.

I entered Noor's room and found her still sobbing and shaking in bed. On hearing my footsteps, she crawled away, facing the wall.

"Did you sleep last night?" I asked her.

She remained quiet.

"Crying is not going to help you," I said, deciding it was time to tear off my façade of goodness. "If you don't stop whimpering, I'll ask Shiva uncle to come back with his clown mask."

She turned at me with folded hands. Her face had become red from weeping all night, her cheeks streaked and crusted. Kaveri came in with a glass of hot milk and glanced at us. Without saying a word, she placed the glass on the table. She was about to leave when Noor caught her pallu. The girl broke into tears.

"Save me," she muttered, "aunty, please."

Kaveri looked at me nervously. Then she pulled her pallu free and quickly walked away.

"Should I call Shiva uncle?" I asked Noor.

"No...please, I beg of you," she shook her head, "no, please-"

"Then wipe your eyes and listen to me."

"Please," she pleaded, trembling.

"Listen," I demanded. "Today is your last chance. If you want to see your mom, learn a verse from the Koran."

I left her sniffling on the bed as I walked out.

A few hours later, the Arabic teacher, a short and fidgety man, invited me to the room where Noor was kept. The girl stood against the wall, her hands joined over her stomach. She had stopped shedding tears. Perhaps she accepted that this was the only way to reunite with her mother.

"She is ready," the teacher beamed. "She is a brilliant student. Noor *beti*, start."

"Wait," I said, "Noor, wear your burqa and hold the Koran in your hands. In front, like this. I will bring the Handycam."

All arrangements done, Noor started her recitation in Arabic. Her lips curled into exaggerated pouts as her head wobbled up and down. I had not expected her to pick up so soon the hills and valleys of the language that I disliked from the core of my heart. However, she displayed excellent memory and occasionally glanced up at the ceiling to recall the subsequent flow of sentences. She blurted out the wrong words a few times, and the Arabic teacher corrected her from the side-line. His voice needed to be edited out, I noted in my mind. I could not understand the Arabic portion but noticed the teacher nod in appreciation and encouragement. Then she translated the verses into English.

"Good and evil deeds are not equal," she said. "Repel evil by what is better; then you will see that who was once your enemy has become your dearest friend."

"So verily with the hardship, there is a relief," she said next, "verily with the hardship, there is a relief."

And then, "Women of purity are for men of purity and men of purity are for women of purity."

"Truly, it is not their eyes that are blind," she took a pause and added in a voice clear as water, "but their hearts."

She ended with, "Indeed we belong to Allah, and indeed to Him we will return."

She kept on blinking innocently at the camera even after I had stopped recording. I gave her a thumbs-up, indicating the job was finished. She returned to her bed. I paid the Arabic teacher his dues, adding extra cash to assure myself that he would keep his mouth shut. Although I knew that he loved his six grandchildren enough not to cause any trouble.

Then I informed Noor that we would enjoy a special feast for dinner to celebrate her growth into a pukka Mussalman. Tomorrow we will start for her home. In reply, her face lit up, but she said nothing. Her trust in me was wounded beyond repair.

One of her verses kept coming back to me as I left her.

"So verily with the hardship, there is a relief; verily with the hardship, there is a relief."

I wondered if causing hardships to others brought me relief. Going into Kaveri's room, I told her to keep her door bolted in the night and not come out even if she heard screams. She asked no questions. She nodded. I was confident she would yet again perform the duty of a good wife.

Poor Noor, I thought. She had no idea what torments awaited her tonight.

Chapter 13

Riju

Aziza and I waited at the Kolkata airport for our flight to Mumbai. Aziza was filling up the time by playfully chasing a little girl who ran around in the open space of the lobby.

Soon the girl bent before her brother, a toddler, and puffed out her cheeks. The boy, advancing tiny fingers, popped her cheeks, and both of them burst into giggles. Their father lifted them in his arms and disappeared into a corridor as Aziza looked at them silently.

"What happened?" I asked Aziza.

"Nothing."

"Did she remind you of your childhood?"

"No," she kneaded her fingers for a while. "Her father made me remember something that my father never did." She did not say anything more, perhaps refusing to let out her emotions.

"I see," I said and decided not to pursue the topic any further since it was getting too personal.

"What about your parents?" she asked me, "Where are they?"

"Pilgrimaging to Badrinath," I said. "They keep frequenting religious places, saying that it would prolong the lives of their sons. But I think the actual reason is that they love travelling."

"Is your father retired?"

"Yes. He was in the Indian army."

"And your mother?"

"She was a nurse," I said. "First in Bangladesh, then in India."

She gave me a curious look.

"She used to work in an army hospital in Bangladesh," I explained. "My father met her during the 1971 war. He was injured. She nursed him back to health. They got married, resulting in my father almost losing his job. But then he managed...well, it's a long story."

"Very romantic," she said. However, hints of glumness still lingered on her face. Maybe to distract herself, she ventured into a different topic by asking if my father inspired me to join the IPS. I said that she was right. I did not tell her I felt cathartic when I put a criminal behind bars. I contributed to solving the complex, invisible Rubik's cube of the world's behaviour, which was being set into order bit by bit. We, the protectors of society, helped the builders of society focus on making advancements without worrying about safety.

Presently a piece of breaking news came upon a plasma screen in front of us. Although the TV was muted, running sentences at the bottom declared that the second video of Noor had been released on YouTube.

Aziza stared at me, her eyes frozen by anxiety and fear. Bitterness settled around my tongue. Pushing aside the questions crowding in my mind, I played the video on my phone.

Noor, in that same extravagant burqa, stood stiffly against a bedsheet. She recited verses in Arabic that Aziza told me were from the Koran. Although the girl held the holy book in her hand, she did not peer inside it. She had memorized the verses. Her mechanical sentences made it clear that she spoke without interest, under impulsion. She faltered and stammered on several occasions. Many a time, she shook her head and started over laboriously. She then repeated the verses in English. After pausing for a moment on her face, the video ended.

Aziza buried her face in her hands, mumbling, "Allah, ya Allah."

None of us spoke for a long time. Words failed me as thoughts took over my mind. I could not erase the last image of the video from my memory. Terror eclipsed Noor's big eyes, and colour vanished from her face. Hope had abandoned her muscles; she struggled to push saliva down her throat as she spoke.

"Someone made her undergo a crash course in Arabic," I muttered, although I knew anyone could have figured it out.

"This," Aziza said, looking up, "I am afraid, is sure to make many people's blood boil."

"She stumbled many times while speaking," I remarked, seeking relief in staying with my own line of thoughts. It, however, did not make me feel any better. I had witnessed numerous crimes. And the curse of a secret operator had kept me silent because I had orders of doing nothing except pass on information to higher authorities. My duties had forced me to build an armour against emotions. But now, that shield was cracking. I felt a sudden surge of desperation. I had to save Noor, for her sake, and for mine.

The previous video had been taken down by YouTube within two hours of its release because it had offended religious sentiments. I downloaded this clip through a screen-recording app to watch it whenever we wanted. I played it three more times, holding my breath on every occasion. Then I went for a stroll.

"Before you rush out in search of the right answer," a professor in the RAW training department used to say, "ask yourself, have you found the right question?"

Were we asking the right question?

When I returned, half an hour remained before we boarded our flight. I pulled Aziza to an empty corner beside a closed shop.

"Why do you think Noor is stumbling so often while reciting the verses?" I asked her.

"That's easy," she said. "She has learnt the surahs, I mean the verses, for the first time, at least in Arabic. So naturally, her pronunciation is all over the place, and she even ends up blurting out irrelevant words."

"It's because she's a beginner. But the kidnapper could have made her rehearse it multiple times before the recording. If he intended her to be flawless, he could have even written the words, prompting her from behind the camera."

She ran a hand over the bandage on her neck and looked away. She looked exhausted. "Maybe he did not want her to be perfect."

"But why?"

"I don't know." She raised her hands, then let them fall down by her sides.

"What he wanted everyone to see her flaws?" I said. "The way a Muslim girl falters in reciting the verses shows how far she is from being a true Muslim. It is a slap on the face of the traditional Muslim culture, isn't it?"

"If that's the case, then it's unfortunate," she said. "Oh, she was so nervous that she had to stop herself from shaking. Riju..." she paused.

"Hmm?"

"I think he is going to kill her." Her lips trembled. "I can't forget the face of that poor child for one moment. The senseless way in which she fumbled and...something else struck me as strange."

"What?" I asked.

"She was tutored in other words of Arabic as well," she said. "Her stray words were inappropriate, alright, but they were still meaningful words."

"Okay, that can be a coincidence. Or not. Tell me more about these words?"

Aziza asked me to play a particular section of the video.

"See here," she paused the video, "Noor was supposed to say, "*Fa-Inna maAAa alAAusri yusra*", but instead of '*alAAusri,*' she says, '*alkuhuf*'. Then she quickly corrects herself."

"What does '*alkuhuf*' mean?" I asked.

"Caves."

"That does not make any sense," I said.

"There's more, listen, here she should say, "*biha fa-innaha la tamAAl-absaru walakin*", but in the place of '*tamAAl*', she says, '*alzalam*', which means 'darkness'. However, she starts over from the beginning, using the right word this time around."

"Caves, darkness. It sounds absurd."

"Again," she went back to a previous point in the video, "here the *surah* goes, "*Inna maAAa alAAusri yustra*," but in place of '*maAAa*', Noor says, '*masjid*'."

At last, an Arabic word that I understood.

"And one more, where is it?" She searched and found what she was looking for. "Yes, here. Again Noor falters and says '*alfil*' at the beginning of the phrase '*fa-itha al-lathee*'. '*Alfil*' is Arabic for 'elephant'."

"And yet again, she corrects herself," I said. "Are there any more wrong words?"

Aziza shook her head. "She stumbles a lot. But these are the only different words she uses in the whole video which are meaningful."

"Caves, darkness, mosque, and elephant." I dropped my phone back in my pocket. "Is she trying to tell us something through these mistakes?"

Aziza shrugged, "I don't' think so. I think they were honest slipups."

"But what if they are not?"

"Riju, she's not a grown-up."

"She might be more intelligent than we think," I insisted. "See, straight up, there is a connection in her misplaced words. The caves of Elephanta. And maybe she was describing those caves as 'dark.'"

"Are you sure you are not reading too much into the errors of a small girl?"

"Perhaps I am," I said. "But am I being completely unreasonable?"

"Still, it seems too far-fetched. Surely, she's not kept somewhere near the Elephanta caves. There are only a few residential houses there. And as far as I know, the island does not have a mosque either."

"Maybe she wanted us to understand two separate phrases."

"Or three, or four," Aziza said, irritation rising in her voice. "Or maybe none. For all we know, there might be no meaning in it whatsoever. What if Noor went to the zoo, saw elephants, and described them as dark-complexioned?"

I grew silent.

"There could be endless possibilities if we try to find logic in randomness," Aziza, perhaps thinking that she had been a bit rude, added softly.

There was every chance that she was right. I was behaving like a doctor who imagined diseases in perfectly healthy people. I was over-suspicious, true, but it was my job, my character.

The boarding started. We joined the queue. Patterns formed then fell apart in my head, the pieces unable to hold together. They went all the way back to lessons from my cryptography classes, but then I realized that it was ridiculous. Noor could never have known about such patterns. I must lower the complexity level, I decided. The connection, if there was one, should be simple.

It was not before we had taken our seats in the flight that the solution struck me.

"Noor is a smart girl," I whispered to Aziza. "In a very subtle way, she communicated two phrases. 'Elephanta caves' and 'dark mosque'."

She looked at me, puzzled, waiting for me to finish or realize that I did not make any sense.

"Which," I added, "stands for 'Andheri mosque'."

I leaned back in my chair while the plane taxied towards the runway. I closed my eyes, letting them fill up with long-suppressed sleep.

Chapter 14

Vikram

I waited till everyone fell asleep, and the bungalow grew silent. I did not worry about getting out of bed unnoticed since Kaveri slept in a separate room. She had long ago resigned to the fate of spending her life with an unloving husband. However, she never denied me when I sometimes, driven by the urge of her lithe body, would climb on her and take off her clothes. We would have sex without talking. I would ignore her ageing skin and the vanishing curves of her waist. Over time, I had stopped hearing even the sounds of sharp breaths coming from her. After the perfunctory act, I would wear my pyjamas. She would study me as though trying to solve a puzzle, understand me. She would not even touch her clothes until I had gone out of sight.

I could not care less for what she thought of me. I had brought her enough respect and wealth to compensate for a sorrowful married life. On the contrary, I was surprised that she did not get naked when I entered her room at night. Wasn't that what a slave would do?

Video camera in hand, I now picked my way through the darkness, towards the room where Noor was locked up. I left Shiva out of this because I did not want anyone to watch my most vulnerable side, my ugliest side. Also, his loyalty might break down from the smell of young flesh.

Losing restraint, he might try to grab a share of the girl. No, I would not let it happen. Noor was mine. She was the atonement for my failure to save *pitaji*.

And she was about to save this country.

Strangely, my heart began to beat faster as I reached her doorstep. After all the necessary crimes I had committed, I had expected this to feel like another service to society. But no, this was special, I reminded myself. This was the tipping point, the final push that I had been waiting for since forever. Once the rape video of Noor was released, the Muslims would turn into maniacs. Nothing would stop them from leaping into a battle that they were incapable of winning. Without a doubt, some Hindu lives would be lost, yes, but they would be worshipped as martyrs.

Who said collateral damage had no religion?

I walked inside the darkroom and shut the door behind me. I could not hear anything but the fragrance of rose attar was unmistakeably strong. Ah, I thought, how arousing.

"Noor," I whispered, "are you asleep?"

Thoughts of her tender body had already made me hard. I imagined her vigorous attempts to flee from my grips and me overpowering her, my Muslim organ plundering hers, again and again. The pictures gave me goose-bumps. My heart went mad as I searched for the switchboard.

"Noor," I called out as the light came on.

The bed lay empty.

The video camera would have dropped from my hand had my fingers not frozen around it.

"Noor!" I shouted, running inside the attached bathroom. "Where are you?"

There was no one in the bathroom. Noor's burqa hung from a hook – she had left it behind as a blob of spit on my face. The window was shut, and besides, it was guarded by solid grills. Where did she go? And how? I felt so shocked that I collapsed on the floor. If I lost her, my life would become hell. I struggled to climb back up on my feet. I phoned Shiva.

"Noor has escaped," I told him in a voice cracked by dread. "You search the outhouse and the garden. I will look inside the bungalow. Be very careful, don't involve the security men. We must find her, right now, or else..." Unable to complete the sentence, I disconnected the mobile.

It took me a moment to realize what had happened. I hurried out of the room and moved along the corridor. My legs felt cramped, muscles stiff, as the thrill that had occupied them was replaced by fright. My heart still thumped, only now its engine was anxiety, not lust. The invisible chains of age slowed me down.

I dragged myself into Kaveri's bedroom. She was wide awake, seated on her bed, her figure lit by a bedside lamp. Her crooked smile, which I had not seen for several years, cleared the clouds of doubt in my mind.

"*Saali haraamzaadi!*" I screamed and charged at her. I clutched her throat and pinned her to the bed, mounting her. "Why did you do it, you bitch?"

Her smile evaporated. Gurgles of pain emerged from her mouth. She was not speaking, the bitch. For a moment, I thought she remained silent out of habit. I wrapped her pallu around her neck and pulled it.

"How dare you?" I hissed.

She clutched my wrists and twisted them. My hands came away more because of the surprise from her first display of courage than anything else. She crawled away, coughing, and settled on the far edge of the bed. She panted, fighting for breath. A strange sound came out from her throat, and before I realized it, it grew into a burst of laughter which led to more coughing.

"You-ahh, you," when she started speaking, her voice was calm, "you are losing your strength. You have become old."

I could not respond; this animal, whom I had mistaken as a tamed creature. I fed it for numerous years. My pet had suddenly become bold enough to turn around and bite her master. And she stared back. Today her eyes did not try to understand why a person like me existed in this world. Today they burnt with disgust and triumph.

"Where is she?" I demanded. "Tell me now."

"Your grey hair is turning white."

"Where is she?"

"I don't know," she said, her defiant smile making a comeback.

"Now!" I shouted.

She did not flinch. "I don't know."

"You..." I chased her and, as she tried to wriggle away, caught her feet. She kicked away my hand. Both her mind and her body had become rebelliously strong today.

"Tell me now, or I will call Shiva," I warned.

"Call whoever you want," she snapped. "The truth is, I don't know where she went."

"You have hidden her somewhere, *saali kutiya*. Where?"

"What words, mister ex-governor, *wah*," she jeered. "Once Noor left, I shut the door and turned away. I was positive that you would force it out of me if I knew which direction she went. So there you have it, I have as much idea about her whereabouts as you do."

"Liar. You liar bitch." I surprised her with a quick burst of movement and thrust her against the wall. I again started to throttle her with her pallu. "You are lying."

"I am not," she managed through sputtering breaths, "and...ahh...if you kill me, then...ahh..."

I had not thought of it before. If I harmed Kaveri, there would be more trouble. Her father was a Supreme Court judge, and her mother was a senior diplomat. The exact reasons I married her now came back to haunt me. If I hurt my wife, her family would spread enough dirt to keep me away from any public involvement.

I let her go and came out of her room. I took long breaths, hoping they would bring a calming effect. I had to regain my composure because a bad temper would keep me from reasoning. I rang up Shiva again.

"Did you find her?" I asked.

"No, Sir," he said. "She is not in the garden."

"How is it possible? Had she tried to cross the fence, the security would have caught her."

"Do you think she is still in the compound?"

"She must not have gone too far," I said. "Did you check the backyard?"

"That's where I am right now."

"Fine," I said. "Don't forget the outhouse. Noor is here, Shiva; I can sense it."

I next called the guards at the main entrance. I gave them a false story, saying that my wife had seen a girl lurking outside her window. They said that they had not noticed any trespasser.

"Sir, the night is quiet as usual," the head of security said. "Not even a dog is roaming anywhere in the periphery."

I instructed him to keep his eyes open. If they found a girl, they must bring her to me without any delay. The sight had terrified my wife, I added before hanging up.

It struck me as strange. Had Kaveri left Noor outside the front door, someone would have spotted her. The fences of my house rose considerably high. They must have stopped Noor from climbing over. What was I missing? I was still lost in the puzzle when I received a call back from the head of security.

"Sir, we did some extra rounds," he said. "We caught a beggar, a boy, wandering on the other side of the road."

"My wife saw a girl, around ten years old," I said, irritated. "What will I do with a boy?"

"We stopped him because he seemed suspicious. He has a brand new teddy bear in his sack. It looks expensive."

"Teddy bear, oh." It must be Baadshah, I thought. "What colour is it? Can you check its label?"

"One minute. It says Hamley's."

"Un-huh," I tried to sound casual, "no harm in checking someone who appears suspicious. Make him wait. I want to see him." I ended the conversation and was about to redial Shiva when I heard Kaveri's voice behind.

"She is such a kind girl," she said.

I turned around. My wife was leaning against the wall beside the door of her room.

"Noor felt bad throwing it away," she continued, "the teddy. So she gave it to a beggar before leaving."

I should calmly deal with Kaveri this time around, I told myself.

"Why are you doing this?" I asked in a subdued tone. "Why are you not speaking the truth?"

"But I told you the truth."

I shook my head. "You said that you left her outside the door. If it was true, she could not have disappeared from the campus. Please, Kaveri, tell me, where have you kept her?"

She went on looking at me, her smile resurfacing bit by bit.

"Along with your strength, your intelligence is also fading away," she said. "Otherwise, you would have remembered that I did not mention outside which door I left her."

I did not know if I should trust her.

"Today evening, I went out shopping in our Fiat," she added, "I took Noor with me, and I last saw her outside the door of our car."

"But-"

She held out a hand.

"Thank you for providing a roof over my head all these years," she said. "Tomorrow onwards, you don't have to worry about that. I am leaving. I will stay with my parents."

"You could have left without a word. Without causing this *tamasha*."

"It's not a *tamasha*," she said quietly, "it was necessary to save the girl and ruin you."

"Ruin me? You think that she can ruin me? Even if she talks, who will believe her?"

"I think she will find a way." She turned around, stepping away. "And to ensure her success, I gave her a parting gift. The package that you had so carefully kept in the locker. I assume it was something important?"

At first, I thought Kaveri was joking. I tried to make her deny it because I felt too uneasy about going and checking it myself. But she relapsed into her characteristic quietness, which now seemed to have changed its colour. It was no more submissive; it had grown into obstinacy.

As she retreated into her room, I thought of her naivety. She did not know how many ways I could punish her without letting my name get in the muck. But all that could wait for now. I must see if the antique box was still safe. I had planned on delivering it to Dr Tharoor the next day. He had arranged a secret place in ISRO to keep it till he began his experiments.

Anxiety coursing in my blood, I went inside the locker room. Everything looked normal from the outside. I unlocked the chest, pulled out the drawer, and peered inside.

It was empty.

For an instant, I thought I had gone blind. Then I realized Kaveri did not lie. The parcel had disappeared. Suddenly I felt as though the darkness of the night had seeped into my chest.

Chapter 15

Riju

Aziza and I had to tip off the police about the places that Noor mentioned in her video. Aziza said she would anonymously call Dhritiman and let him know. We used a public booth outside the airport to avoid getting detected by a CCTV camera.

"Did he find the information interesting?" I asked her once she had placed the phone back on its hook.

"From his voice, it appeared as though he jumped off his chair."

"Good," I said, relieved. "I am certain Dhritiman will contact the teams in Mumbai right away."

Aziza and I decided against staying with any acquaintance. Dropping even a hint about our intentions in Mumbai could prove dangerous. So we booked two rooms at the T24 Residency hotel near Airport Road. Then, sitting in my room, we discussed our next steps. I suggested we visit either the Elephanta caves or the Andheri Chakala mosque, the most famous mosque in the area. We would ask if anyone had seen Noor or heard something from her.

However, I admitted, the possibility of finding anything worthwhile was faint. Every day thousands of people thronged to both landmarks. Anyone spotting Noor and remembering her face amidst a sea of faces seemed unlikely. I made up my mind to call Dhritiman again. I must enquire if the police had any new information. But I had to be cautious, I reminded myself. I could not afford Dhritiman to get suspicious of me.

"But which one should we target first?" I asked Aziza.

"Why, of course, the Elephanta caves," she said and swallowed a painkiller.

"Is it still hurting a lot?" I pointed at her bandaged wound.

In trying to shake her head, she winced from the pain. "I don't think the nurse has done it properly. But I will be fine."

"I can give it a fresh dressing," I offered. "I have some experience in it."

She produced an antibiotic solution, bandages, and two cotton rolls from her bag. As I drew towards her, I did not fail to notice her slightly stale breaths and tired eyelids.

"Why not the mosque?" I asked her while replacing the cotton. "It's nearer. And it will be a smaller area to cover."

"I am assuming the kidnapper made Noor wear a burqa when they went out. It is easier to hide her face that way. And...ah."

"Sorry, it's almost done," I said. "And?"

"It is more difficult to remember the face of a girl in a mosque if she is wearing a burqa."

"Fair point," I said. "Noor would be more noticeable in the Elephanta caves."

"The ferry opens at half-past nine," she checked her watch. "We can start now for the Gateway of India."

I observed the weary look on her face. She clearly needed some rest. For a moment, I considered feigning tiredness myself and suggesting we took a nap for half an hour. Would she refuse? Then I grew conscious of every second ticking by. Every breath that Noor took in the clutches of her captor pushed her nearer to doom. Moreover, if we reached the caves before the Mumbai police did, we would prevent ourselves from getting entangled in further complications.

"Let's go," I said.

Underneath a delightful sky, the ocean was draped like a quilt over the surface of the earth. The only disturbances were caused by the ferries that pushed off from the Gateway of India and the steamers whose horns failed to break my thoughts about Noor's kidnapping. How was it possible that the passengers on two sides of a train compartment saw different persons – a man and a woman – carry the girl away? The darkness helped the perpetrator for sure, but how could the witnesses be divided in what they saw? The solution to the problem eluded me as we ran out of any other leads we could follow.

Aziza and I reached the island.

Aziza, who had been rather chirpy through the ferry ride, got into the toy train that transported visitors into the island's interiors. The journey ended at the foot of the hill from which the climb towards the caves began. A wide staircase hopped up along the slope. On both sides, rows of shops were busy selling knick-knacks – crystal necklaces, Ganesh carved from betel nuts, minakari bangles, key-chains, wild berries, boulders of semi-precious stones, hand paintings, refrigerator magnets with Mumbai scenery embossed on them, and sunglasses. Many of them were priced under a hundred bucks. The shopkeepers laid them out with careful precision.

"We have to be secretive about our questions," I told Aziza. "So choose a local person wisely."

The cacophonous storekeepers filled the air with promises of reasonable price. They spoke in Hindi when the Indians passed by and beckoned the foreigners in English.

"Madam," a seller called out to a blonde woman who made the mistake of glancing at his shop, "top quality Indian umbrella. Full mirror-work. Lowest price. O madam, this way, please."

"Gemstone rings, madam," said another man, "tiger-stones, rubies, corals, pokhraj, natural crystals. All originals."

"Here, please, madam," motioned the first one, "I said, please."

"This side madam, breakfast," called out a neighbouring food-seller, "vada pav, misal pav, samosa pav, bhajji pav, bhel puri, batata puri. Not spicy at all, no stomach problem. And refreshing drinks. Tender coconut water, lemon soda, masala soda, jaljeera…"

The blonde gave them a gentle smile and departed, her suntanned legs shuffling hurriedly.

We approached the food-seller. I played Noor's latest video on my phone, but he failed to recognize her. A few steps ahead, a man was admonishing a monkey that had snatched away his packet of peanuts.

Then, Aziza touched my hand, gesturing me to stop. She pointed towards a dark-skinned woman squatting behind piles of printed T-shirts. She swept her arm over her products, covering her eyes with a hand.

"*Loot lo mujhe,*" the woman screamed, "*loot lo*, rob me."

Aziza, wearing a quizzical look, went near the shop. Seeing this, the woman clasped her hand over her eyes more tightly and shouted again, "*Utha lo*, whatever you want, just pick it up and leave. Rob me. I won't even call the security guards."

Aziza began to laugh. "What do you mean?" she asked.

"Madamji," the shopkeeper lady did not uncover her eyes, "my eyes are shut. Take whatever you like before I change my mind."

"But what is the price of this T-shirt?"

"Only 150 rupees, madam. Pick any. I am not looking. Because I am giving it away for so cheap, it is as good as getting robbed."

"Then why are you selling it for so cheap?"

"Madamji," the woman said, "please don't ask questions. *Jaldi, jaldi,* take everything." She shouted to the passers-by, "*Loot lo, loot lo, idhar se. Utha lo, paisa nahi chahiye.* I don't want money."

As though on cue, a scrawny young man picked up a T-shirt and looked at the woman for a second. Then he began to put on the garment over the shirt he was wearing.

"*Abbe halkat!*" the shopkeeper lady screamed and jumped up on her feet. "Why are you wearing it? Did you buy it?"

"I-I-" the young man scrambled for words. "Aren't you inviting people to rob you?"

"Are you from the moon? Why would I give them away for free?"

"I thought-"

"You thought I couldn't see anything?" she pointed two fingers at her own eyes. "These are sharper than a barber's scissors. I see everything. Now either pay for that T-shirt or put it down."

"Arre," the young man held up his palms, "I was just checking the size."

"Is that how you check the size? *Pagal hai kya?*" she gestured towards me. "Ask this good saabji to hold it on your back like a curtain. Then you'll know if it fits. Anyway, you need a smaller size."

The young man dropped the T-shirt and hurried away without looking at me.

"*Kahan kahan se namoone aa jaate hain*," she turned to Aziza. "Madamji, only the T-shirts in that pile are 200 rupees each, the rest are 150 rupees each. See this, this is my favourite," she hoisted a T-shirt that said: Mumbai meri jaan.

I went and stood beside Aziza.

"Are your eyes really sharp?" I asked the woman.

"Yes, saabji, very sharp."

"Do you remember every person who crosses your stall?"

She chuckled, folding the T-shirt in her hand. "Don't joke now. That is not possible. But I remember many of them. Especially the ones who stand out in the crowd."

I took out Noor's paused video on my phone and showed it to the shopkeeper.

"Do you recall seeing her?" I asked.

"No," she returned the phone and began arranging her products. "What happened to her?"

"She is missing."

"*Aai shappath*, the first time I saw you, I knew you were a policeman."

"I am not a policeman," I said, lowering my voice. "I am this girl's elder brother. We can't find her for two days. Someone informed us that she was spotted here."

"Two days? Then it must be fresh in my memory. *Dikhao,* let me have another look?"

She retook the phone and peered into it. This time she gave it a good look, her eyes sweeping over the picture carefully. In the end, her lips widened into a smile.

"Do you remember seeing her?" Aziza asked.

"No," the woman shook her head, "but I remember seeing her burqa."

"Are you sure it was the same one?" I asked.

"Yes. I mean, look at its embroidery. I get my material from the wholesale market in Crawford's, and even there, you won't find a burqa like this one."

"Did you notice this burqa on a girl or a woman?"

"No, it was a girl. She was this tall." She made gestures with her hands to indicate the height.

"When did you see her?" I asked, my pulses quickening.

"Yes-no, the day before yesterday. Late in the morning."

"And who was she with?"

"Umm, a man was holding her hand. He was big, like, this big. And there was another man, a tall one. They paused in front of my shop for a moment. The girl fed bananas to the monkeys."

"What else?" Aziza said, excitement catching her voice, "What else do you remember seeing about them?"

"Nothing," she shrugged. "Nothing unusual."

"Okay, tell me about the usual things that you saw," I insisted. "What were the men wearing?"

"Ordinary shirts and trousers. And slippers. Oh, they wore big sunglasses, this big."

"Can you guess their ages?"

"The tall man was aged," she replied. "The other one was younger, maybe in his thirties."

"Aged? Was he very old?"

"No. Somewhat old, but his arms looked strong."

"Can you give me an estimate?" I said.

"*Maaf kijiye* saabji," the woman said. "I was busy running my shop. I just caught a glimpse of them."

"Did you see them go up or down?"

"Up."

"And down?"

"I did not see them going down. Saabji, you can tell the police about your lost sister. The police station is near the jetty. Now, please, I have to work. Madamji, you want a T-shirt?"

"Give me three," Aziza said. "And, thank you."

But I could not let it go so quickly. I grew eager to squeeze out every bit of information because our chances of finding Noor became dimmer. I could feel the numbness of despair in my shoulders.

"I am sorry," I said to the shopkeeper-lady, "but this is important. Don't you recall anything else, anything at all?"

The woman packed three T-shirts in a paper bag, transferred them to Aziza, and collected her money.

"Tell me about the hairstyle of the men who accompanied her," I persisted.

She took her place behind her goods and thought for a while. "The older person had grey and black hair. Or was it all grey? And the other one, the heavy man, his hair was, un-huh, I don't remember."

"So one of them had at least some grey hair?"

"I am not sure, saabji."

"What was the colour of their clothes?" I asked. "What did they carry in their hands?"

She shrugged.

"And did you notice their pockets," I went on, "their watches or-"

Aziza stopped me by touching my elbow. "She does not know anything else," she said.

"You don't understand," I moved my arm away, "we don't have any more clues. If we return without anything substantial from here, we have nowhere else to go."

"We still have the mosque."

"The mosque will be of no help."

"We don't know that yet."

"I know it," I started climbing up the stairs. "It was you who said it. No one would notice a girl wearing a burqa in a mosque."

"Let's ask the guides in the caves."

"We can't ask them," I retorted.

She stopped in her tracks. "Why?"

"Because I know Dhritiman," I replied. "He acts fast. And if he has not changed drastically since I last saw him, every certified guide up there is roaming around with Noor's picture in his phone. If we question them, they will become suspicious."

She paused, thinking. "What about the uncertified guides?"

"Dhritiman is not foolish. He would ask the certified guides to involve everyone in the search." All of a sudden, the frustration piling up in me gave way. "It was my mistake bringing you here. I should have known that you have no experience in how criminal cases are handled."

"Excuse me," she said, clearly hurt. "I wanted to come here voluntarily. For you, this might be another 'criminal case' to be solved. For me, it means a lot more than that."

Nothing could be far from the truth. If this was just another case, I would not have risked my safety and my cover for it. I remembered my doubts about Aziza's motivation to rescue Noor.

"Then tell me about it," I demanded. "Tell me why you are here?"

Without answering, she turned away. She resumed her way up the stairs. I followed her silently. We showed Noor's photograph to a couple of hawkers, but they could not provide anything useful. We were about to approach a popcorn seller when we noticed the constables. There were four of them. They were carrying a blown-up printout of Noor's face. Dhritiman was quicker than I had thought. He had passed on Aziza's anonymous information. Also, he had managed to get hard copies of the girl's photo distributed among the constables. And they had already begun their investigation.

"We must leave now," I told Aziza, to which she nodded.

Although I was habituated to stealing short naps whenever possible, I could not get any sleep during our ferry ride back to the Gateway of India. Aziza and I did not speak to each other during the whole journey. I felt a pang of regret for the spell of harsh behaviour towards her. However, I still thought that she was hiding something. I once tried to stick back a corner of her bandage that was coming off, but she pushed away my hand and took care of it herself.

What worried me the most was that we returned empty-handed. This visit had jumbled up the connections in my head more than before. Noor's co-passengers in the train allegedly saw her with a man and a woman. However, according to the shopkeeper-lady outside the Elephanta caves, Noor was accompanied by a pair of men. Were we up against a gang of kidnappers? Why did they bring Noor to the caves? What made them so complacent that they risked getting exposed? The more I tried to think of a future course of action, the more suffocating my despair felt.

I had no clue that I could follow, no more cards to turn over.

Chapter 16

Vikram

Our efforts in the morning had yielded no information on the whereabouts of Noor. Shiva and I had exhausted all ideas, and each one of them had ended in failure.

In the early daylight, I had watched the triumphant, wordless figure of Kaveri walking away. With the help of two aids, she had rolled six massive trolleys till the main gate. I had no idea my wife had so many possessions. All of them had been bought with my money. The backstabber had left in my Fortuner, without even a look back at my bungalow. The woman had put together a pyre for destroying my career and my life. I had never loved her, and I had never been interested to know if she loved me.

I would see her again, I vowed to myself, for one last time. We had scores to settle.

An hour later, Shiva departed to wake up his gang members. They would spread across the whole city, searching for Noor. It was about time my pet gangsters proved their worth. But I could not rely on a group of unorganized goons alone. I had to employ other, more methodical options. Every moment Noor spent away from my sight increased the chances of someone else finding her first.

Last night's occurrences still haunted me as I turned the phone again and again in my hand. I faced a crucial decision. Should I involve the police? True, I had quite a few trustworthy servants in uniform, but they were faithful to my position, not me. They would switch sides when they found out I was about to fall from my throne. Which was why goondas were necessary. They served their masters like dogs, while policemen, like cats, cared only about food and shelter.

But in this situation, I decided I needed every help I could get. Hence, I dialled the number.

"Sahib," Mandeep answered, "what a pleasure. Congratulations on Basirhat riot making it to the front page."

"Commissioner," I said. "Something has gone terribly wrong. I need you to fix it."

"Any problem with the second video?" he sounded concerned, but I knew he was pretending. "I was saying that," he added, "I had ensured that it can't be tracked even with-"

"No," I interrupted, "the video release went as planned. It is something else."

"I see," he paused for a while, then continued, "you already know? But who told you?"

"Know what? Let me finish, please. This is important."

"I am listening."

I struggled to get the words out. "Noor is missing."

There was silence on the other side. My vocal admission heightened the unrest in my chest.

"Last night, my wife took her out and let her run away," I explained.

"But- I was saying that, why did she do it?"

"I don't know."

"Do you know where she left the girl?"

"No."

"This is a huge problem."

"Commissioner," I said, "you must do whatever you can and retrieve her."

"Alright," he said. "I will immediately alert all stations in Mumbai. It will not be a good idea to involve Dhritiman in this. He is, you know, the honest kind. I will bypass him. I can manage it."

"Make sure that when the girl is captured, the news does not spread. She should be brought to me."

"Yes," he said. "I will make it clear that whoever finds Noor informs me directly."

"Also, one more thing. Noor has a package with her, kind of a box. I want it delivered to me unopened, without any damage. Understood?"

"What does it contain?"

"I can't tell you that."

"But-"

"Just do as I said."

"Fine," he said. "Sahib, I was saying that this is a huge problem. This is why the payment also…"

"You will get double the usual amount," I said. "Now, go. No, wait. What was the other news?"

"Other news?"

His puzzlement was fake, I knew.

"You said, "I see, you already know?" What were you referring to?"

"Yes," he said, "I was about to call you for this. Dhritiman knows that the girl is in Mumbai."

"How?" I asked, surprised.

"I don't know. What's worse, he wants to go public with this information. Apparently, the media is putting too much pressure on the police. He also believes it would force the kidnapper into making a mistake."

"Is he mad?" I said, rising from my chair. "How can he release such sensitive information about a live case?"

"He will take full responsibility for the aftermath," Mandeep said. "He thinks he will catch the criminal before he can react."

"Commissioner, it is necessary that you stop him. On all accounts, you must stop him."

"I was saying that it is his case. If I interfere, it might be in the records."

"You are his superior," I snapped. "Figure it out and get it done."

I disconnected the call. I felt as though water from all sides was closing in on me, as it had many years ago in Paradeep. My carelessness had resulted in this horrible scheme of things. Why didn't I put a lock outside Noor's room? Why did I trust Kaveri?

I began pacing in my room, feeling trapped. Shiva called on my phone and informed me that he had sent out all his men searching for Noor. He assured me that a small girl could not go far in such a short time.

Then I received a call that I was not expecting at all. It was from the South Block of the Secretariat building, the Prime Minister's office. Suryajit had returned from the Global Environment Summit. On learning about the riots in Basirhat, he had called for an emergency meeting today. After talking with the ministers and the Security Advisor, he would like to discuss a few matters. Hence, I was required to reach Delhi immediately.

Five and a half hours later, four guards escorted me into the conference room in the Panchavati, the prime minister's residence. The room's interiors, primarily used for holding informal meetings, had changed little over the years. I could see the final rays of today's sun touch upon the creeper that ran across the window. Its leaves, collages of green, blue and yellow, were turning into the colour of a pomegranate. The room was jovially lit, causing the central wooden table to gleam along its edges.

Suryajit sat across the table, his face frowning, perhaps from worries. I wondered if he expected anything different from his job. Intisar occupied the chair beside me, running a fingertip over a paperweight. The woman displayed grace in every movement.

"How did the summit go?" I asked Suryajit.

"It went better than I had anticipated," he said. "We discussed a new way of measuring the carbon footprints of nations. And something more interesting happened on the sidelines. I will come to it later." He leant forward from his high chair. "Right now, I am tremendously anxious about Basirhat."

"What were the opinions of the ministers?" I asked, referring to his earlier meetings.

"What can they say?" Intisar said, her voice sounding steely from anger. "I attended the meeting. A Muslim girl has been abducted. No one cares. They shrugged their shoulders as though by now we should take a riot taking place every two years in this country for granted."

I looked at the Prime Minister.

"Your unhappiness is understandable," Suryajit told Intisar. "But I must say that it would have been better had you not gotten into a fight with Gaganji. We should be looking for solutions, not create more frictions."

"*Janab,* how could I restrain myself after-"

"Excuse me," Suryajit stopped her, "but time is of paramount importance. Can we discuss the role that Rathoreji can play in this difficult situation?"

"Sorry," Intisar said, "but I think you misunderstood my behaviour." She turned towards me, "Gaganji said that we should next expect an ISIS-style video, where Noor would be beheaded. Don't you think it is an insensitive comment?"

"I agree with Intisarji on this," I told Suryajit.

"So do I," the Prime Minister said. "Don't worry, I will talk to him. Now, the reason why I requested your presence here. Today morning I went on a helicopter survey of Basirhat. What I saw frightened me. Houses and fields were burning. Human bodies and animal carcasses lay scattered around a pond which, I learnt, was poisoned." He shook his head slowly. "It was a horrific sight."

I imagined the scene, and a soothing breeze of happiness passed over my skin. I hid my genuine emotions with some effort and produced a look of concern on my face.

"What are the police and the army doing," I asked, "apart from what the news bulletins show?"

"They have failed miserably," Intisar said. "Even rubber bullets have not protected them against the stones pelted by mobs. It is a bloodbath out there, spreading fast to other regions in the state. All this when the mischief-makers are still restricted to farming tools. Imagine what will happen when the local guns and gas cylinders come out."

"But how could I be of any help here?" I asked Suryajit, sounding confused.

"Rathoreji," he replied, "you have a lot of experience in countering riots. We are eagerly waiting for your suggestions. Also, you must find a way in which Dilon Main Mohabbat can help placate the violence?"

How amusing. *I* was being asked for a solution to the problem.

"As you very well know, our team only works after the unrest has been brought under control. We appear once the worst has passed. We remove the shadows of suspicion and hatred that remain afterwards."

"I understand," Suryajit said, disappointed. "Then this might sound like an unfair request, but can't you make an exception this time around? We will choose the relatively peaceful areas and-" he stopped, perhaps realizing how unreasonable he sounded. "Frankly, I am feeling helpless about the whole scenario."

"Please understand," I said. "I can't risk it. I feel we would fail in making any difference right now. I promise, once the police have diffused the violence, Dilon Main Mohabbat will visit Basirhat and help in bringing back peace."

"Do you have any suggestions to improve the situation?" Intisar asked me.

"Currently, the only solution I can see is rescuing the girl. She is the cause for it all."

We discussed the steps that could be taken to quieten the turbulence for some more time, all of which, I knew, would fail. The videos had worked wonders, I realized. They had turned speculations into certainty, created a divide between the Hindus and the Muslims. At last, Suryajit changed the topic with great reluctance and anxiety.

"Right after the Summit," he said, "I met Faisal Ahmed. He seemed quite keen to revive Pakistan's relationship with India. He wants to visit Kashmir and have a look around and meet me."

"We have been through this before," Intisar said sternly, "no talks with Pakistan until it stops violating the ceasefire."

"Again, I am with Intisarji on this," I said. "We need to be very careful."

"Don't worry," Suryajit said. "I will not take any step without consulting everyone. Personally, though, I feel the time is right. Faisal Ahmed is desperate to prove that he deserved the win in the last election. Nothing can be a bolder move than resuming peace talks with India. We should seize the opportunity." He glanced at the clock that must have been hanging for generations on the wall. He rose from his chair. "I am late for a meeting. I will contact both of you soon."

After he left the room, Intisar turned towards me. "I hope you will not mind if I take a walk with you?"

"Outside," I said, "in the street."

Once I crossed the perimeter of high security that crawled with guards in uniforms and muftis, Intisar caught up with me. She gestured to me to stop in the shade of a gulmohar.

"Is the girl alright?" she asked as she studied the flowering tree.

"Yes," I said, making sure my voice did not carry any hesitation.

"Again, what is her name?"

"Noor."

"Ah, sweet name. A name that's suitable for the newspapers. So, you have planned to rape her several times, or only once before killing her?"

I observed her face, which showed no sign of sympathy. I wondered how she could keep a casual expression even as she spoke of sinister things. It was perhaps one of the most essential qualities of a seasoned politician. And it was partly why I could never be one of them.

"I have not decided it yet," I answered.

"I must say that the two videos pleased me. And you know I am a difficult woman to please."

"Thank you," I said. "But there has been a slight change in the plan. I will not release the final video tonight. It will take two more days."

Her eyes moved across the horizon before they rested on my face. Maybe they searched for signs which were not supposed to be present. Her look felt piercing and, for some strange reason, slightly arousing.

"Is there anything wrong?" she asked.

"The Commissioner," I said. "He said the intelligence department got very close to detecting the source of the video last time. He will contact a different person for the last job."

"This new person, where is he located?"

"Dubai."

"*Janab*," her lips moved slowly, "a master puts one pawn after another after another, building a chain of pawns. The more distance he creates from the pawn carrying out the task, the safer the master feels. But he does not realize that a chain which is longer is also weaker." She took a step closer, and her breath released a cloud of sweet perfume. "You have no idea how long it took me before I finally chose you as my pawn."

I tried to look unaffected by her comment.

"I understand," I said. "I will run thorough background checks and ensure the new person is reliable."

"There is no time left. The Commissioner should take care of it himself."

I nodded, feeling a bubble of uneasiness rise up my throat. If Intisar came to know that Noor had escaped, she would destroy me in no time.

"Two more days?" she asked. "I thought today was perfect."

"It's a slight delay. I don't think it will make any difference."

"I thought you were incapable of such unintelligent words," she shook her head. "Timing is everything. The Prime Minister has just returned from the Summit. Clearly, he is still fumbling in the darkness for solving the Basirhat problem. This is the perfect time to break him."

"But there are two more years till the election. I thought that was what we were building towards."

"You know that I am a greedy woman," she smiled, and it did not look devilish at all. On the contrary, it softened the outline of her sharp jaws, turning her face more innocent. "Once they watch Noor die, the rioters will explode from rage. Lamenting about the position of the Muslims in this country, I will demand Suryajit's resignation."

"But what if it is not enough?"

"It does not matter if he refuses to step down," she made a waving gesture with her hand. "Five important states will have elections shortly. I will make sure that Basirhat gives us as much mileage as possible. And if I want another push before the final elections, what have I kept you for?"

I stayed silent, trying once again to find the trace of a monster on the surface of her skin, but I failed. It must have taken years of practice before she mastered the almost childishly innocent expression she gave now.

"Let's modify the plan," she said. "You molest the girl – Noor – repeatedly. Yes, it will have a more severe impact. And release the first rape video tomorrow."

"I think-"

"I can't let this chance slip away," she cut in. "Just like every day, today I observed the forehead of the Prime Minister closely. And I saw more lines of worries than ever before."

"I saw them too."

"So you agree," she said. "You must also have noticed that Suryajit was too anxious to even mention the package from South Africa. What is its progress? *Sab khairiyat?*"

I felt my toes stiffen up, but I kept my shoulders relaxed and turned squarely towards her. In the book of body postures, openness was considered truthfulness.

"I will give it to the scientist in a few days," I said, stopping my voice from shaking.

"At one point in time, I was thinking about exposing the Prime Minister on the matter of the package."

"How?" I asked.

"By letting the secret out. Once people learn about what he did, it would not matter what excuse he gives."

She was right. People subconsciously focussed on the information that they wanted to be true. And any explanation thereof only resulted in more misunderstanding. If she exposed Suryajit, he would find himself in political quicksand.

"Of course, I will put myself on safe grounds," she added. "I will announce that I became a part of the secret committee so that I could stop it from committing a crime."

"And what about me?"

She laughed. "Why, surely you will be on my side. Together we will script the downfall of the king."

She said the last sentence with a sweet smile; I wanted to trust her. But then, I knew her character better than believing in her.

"Now," she continued, "I have to prepare arguments on why India should not go for dialogues with Pakistan. Resolving the Pakistan issue is on top of my promises for the elections. I will not let Suryajit score any success with it. *Khuda hafiz.*"

Intisar went away. I pondered why I took orders from someone I knew would not hesitate to betray me for selfish gains. Nothing apart from personal motives had kept us attached. I was compelled to follow the wishes of a Muslim woman to eventually wipe out the Muslims from this country. She encouraged me because Muslim killings gave her more weapons to attack the Prime Minister. She assumed it would lay the path for her to the most powerful chair in the country. Just as I was okay with a few Hindus getting killed along the way, she also thought of the murdered Muslims as collateral damage.

However, even the thought of this country's future moving into the hands of a Muslim gave me shudders. Once again, I would be the saviour. For stopping her from winning the elections, I would finish her, but not now. I would wait till the Muslim population became weak and hollow. Then I would chop off its head. Without their leader, they would fall apart. But presently, I must find Noor, lest Intisar got the wind that something was amiss.

Back in the garden of the Panchavati, I found several Ambassador cars with the 'Government of India' plates parked outside.

A chauffeur in white uniform sprung up, giving me a well-practised salute. "On your saarvice, saar."

"Great," I said. "Now tell me in English how fast can you drive to the airport terminal three."

Chapter 17

Riju

The evening traffic slowed down as it squeezed through a tunnel under a flyover on our way back to the hotel. The images of the bullet holes in the Leopold Café were still lingering in my mind. I had taken Aziza to the café for a late lunch in the afternoon. She had begun spotting and counting the bullet holes in the walls – one near the right corner, one beside the old clock, one that missed a glass pane by an inch, and another right behind where we sat. Breaking our spell of silence, we had recounted the horrors of the Mumbai terrorist attack. The shooters had entered the café and had fired guns without warning, killing several innocents within minutes. Or seconds? How slow had time passed during the blind shooting?

Now Aziza and I were back on talking terms. As our vehicle halted before a traffic signal, she drew my attention to a group of street performers on the pavement. Under the guidance of a straggly woman, four children were enacting a mythological episode, begging for alms. The children from the streets were dressed up as different characters – I could not identify all of them – with their bright clothes torn in several places.

"Do you know which event they are portraying?" Aziza asked me.

I shook my head. "I would be astonished if you tell me that you are interested in Hindu mythology."

"Why do you think I visited Taaki during Durga puja? By the way, I can also teach you a few things about Greek mythology."

I smiled at her appreciatively and pointed my chin at the children. "What are they dramatizing?"

"The legend of Lord Shiva's Ardhanarishvara avatar. Look at him, with the chakra; he is Vishnu. The girl over there is Parvati. That boy is the demon who, smitten by Parvati's beauty, tried to kidnap her. And the remaining boy, the one dressed in strange clothes, is Ardhanarishvara. He is half Shiva, half Parvati."

The demon broke into a dance before Parvati, wishing to impress her. His body moved rhythmically while Vishnu and Ardhanarishvara waited for their turns. Parvati tried to ignore the monster, who responded with more vigorous steps. Parvati became visibly irritated. As she was about to run away from the devil, he seized her hand. With a burst of loud, body-shaking laughter, he pulled her towards him. After a struggle, again displayed through dance, Parvati managed to free her hand. She exited the circle of street light, which acted as the spotlight for the play, and Ardhanarishvara replaced her. Half of this God's body was painted blue, while the other half was covered in white. He wore a leopard printed cloth on one side of his waist with a sari draped across the other half of his body.

On seeing this strange half male, half female form, the demon was shocked. They began another dance, moving around each other but never touching, as though talking through dramatic movements of their limbs. It looked absurd and graceful at the same time.

"The demon," Aziza said, "after finding out that Shiva and Parvati are inseparable, will lose interest in her."

In a moment, the villain, looking dejected, walked away from the scene, and his place was taken up by Vishnu. As he raised his hands skywards and slipped into a devotional dance, our cab began moving.

"Isn't it romantic," Aziza said, "the idea of two hearts uniting in love, becoming parts of the same body?"

I nodded but did not answer her, for a sudden idea had taken birth in my mind. I let it mature, attempting to turn it into a complete picture. It broke apart repeatedly. I wondered if there was any possibility present in it. And then, once I saw it, I grew so excited that I could not speak for a while.

"Aziza," I said, at last, my throat feeling parched. "You have helped me find it."

"Find what?" she said, surprised.

"The solution."

"I don't understand a word of what you are saying."

"You will," I said. "Give me a moment."

I took out my phone and browsed through a few articles and pictures on the internet. Once assured, I called Dhritiman. He picked up the phone, and I asked him if he knew about the legend of Ardhanarishvara.

"No," he replied, perplexed.

"Read up about it on the internet. For now, however, it is sufficient if you know that Ardhanarishvara is half Shiva and half Parvati."

"Riju," he said impatiently, "I am swamped right now. I am making arrangements so that I can look over the investigation in Mumbai myself."

"Hear me out," I insisted. "What I am saying has a strong connection with the case."

"Yaar, but you are talking about Ardhanarnari."

"Ardhanarishvara," I corrected him.

"Yes."

"He is half male, half female."

"You mentioned that," he said. "Shiva and Parvati."

"No. This time I am talking about the person who kidnapped Noor."

"What!" his voice was laden with more disbelief than shock. "You mean he has characteristics of a male and a female? How do you know that?"

"Wrong," I said. "The culprit was dressed up as the modern form of Ardhanarishvara. He wore the clothes of a man on one half of his body and-"

"The dress of a woman on the other half," Dhritiman completed my sentence. His breaths were getting louder. "But it sounds too absurd."

"Think about what your witnesses mentioned," I said. "It is dark. Suppose someone wearing such clothes walks through the corridor in a train compartment. In that case, the people on the one side will think that a man passed by and the witnesses on the other side will confuse him for a woman. Yes or no?"

"I am still having trouble visualizing it, yaar. Wouldn't the person stand out?"

"Not if the dress is designed smartly enough. Again, go on the internet, look through how convincing such a disguise can seem. Of course, it needs the correct make-up. The first man – the short bony man – played a small part in the process. His only jobs were to make Noor sit in the train and ensure that the bulbs did not light up that evening."

"But- okay, leave it. Go on."

"The big man," I said, "the real kidnapper wore a contemporary half and half dress so that no one gets suspicious."

"What if someone saw him from the front?"

"He risked it. Listen, this is my theory. He sat nearby in normal clothes and kept an eye on Noor. At night when the lights were out, he followed Noor to the toilet and somehow made her unconscious. After that, he changed into his special clothes."

"And then, how did he hide from the crowd at the Dadar station?"

"He didn't hide. You find numerous freakishly dressed people in the station asking for alms. Many of them even carry a baby or a child apparently dozing off."

He stayed silent for a few seconds, most probably running my story in his mind, eliminating loopholes.

"It is possible," he agreed finally. "You are right; it is quite possible."

"So, we must find him. Get your team to examine CCTV footage from Dadar station. Now that we know what we are looking for, it should be easy. Although it might be more difficult to get a clear view of his face."

"I will start the probe immediately," he said. "By the way, how did you arrive at this crazy idea?"

"You can say that I got lucky. And then I applied something that you don't have."

"What?"

"Brain cells."

"Arrey yaar," he chuckled.

"Okay, I will go now. Tell me later what you find out."

"Goes without saying."

I had almost ended the call when I heard his voice again.

"...wait," he said, "I forgot to mention something. Hello? Are you there?"

"Yes," I said.

"Look, I know you wanted me to keep the information that Noor was seen in Mumbai a secret. But my team thought otherwise in the meeting. So we are announcing it."

I was taken aback. "Why, it's a big mistake. There was a reason behind-"

"I know, I know. But the pressure of the media is becoming too suffocating, yaar. And people here have started attacking us, accusing us of laziness. I had to let some pressure off my shoulder."

"Don't do it, please."

"It's already done," he said. I could almost picture him shrugging. "I just finished the press conference. You will see, it will work in our favour."

I let out a sigh of disappointment. I thought about debating with Dhritiman but realized it would be futile. It would not change what had already happened. Now I desperately hoped that his action would not explode on our faces.

"Call me when you hear back from the surveillance team," I said and hung up.

I looked at Aziza.

"Where one road ends, another one starts," she said. "When are you telling Dhritiman that I helped you in arriving at the explanation?"

"Never," I said. "But that does not change the fact that you have been a great support."

"Finally, a compliment," she said.

She peered out of the window, watching dusk-shrouded buildings pass by, sometimes quickly, sometimes lazily.

"Why did he put so much effort into the kidnapping?" she asked without looking back. "It would have been easier for him to drive her in a personal car."

"Each method of kidnapping comes with its own risks," I said. "Sometimes cameras at toll booths can give the criminal away. Even if he avoids the highway, he must take breaks. The best option is a change of transports, which the kidnapper chose on this occasion. I guess Noor was taken to the Howrah railway station by road. Maybe she was told that her mother was admitted in a hospital far away."

We reached the T24 Residency and went into our separate rooms. I told Aziza that I might wake her up if I received a call from Dhritiman with any fresh news. I lay down on the bed. A hint of sleep had almost shut my eyelids when I opened them again. I wondered how Noor was passing another night away from the safety of her mother.

Chapter 18

Vikram

The early morning news told me that the Commissioner had failed to stop Dhritiman from announcing in the press that Noor was last spotted in Mumbai. I was surrounded by incapable and careless people. And my hands were tied. I could not scream at the Commissioner because I needed his help finding Noor. I already rued visiting the mosque and the Elephanta caves with Noor. I hoped I would not have to pay for those mistakes.

However, after about an hour, another news brightened my mood a bit. Because of the police announcement earlier, people started guessing that the videos of Noor were shot in Mumbai. Which in turn gave rise to violence across two chawls in Chunabhatti and Masjid Bander. A Muslim constable, overtaken by a fit of rage, smashed all the furniture in his police station. In Vashi railway station, unknown perpetrators ripped down the signboards hanging over the platforms, which read:

"The Allah of Islam is the same as the God of Christians and the Ishwar of Hindus."

-Mahatma Gandhi

"The scriptures of Christians, Mussalmans and Hindus are all replete with the teaching of ahimsa."

-Mahatma Gandhi

"Tolerance for other faiths imparts to us a truer understanding of our own."

-Mahatma Gandhi

My phone rang. I had expected a call from Shiva, but instead, Intisar's number appeared on the screen.

"It is unsafe to talk like this, I know," her voice sounded uncharacteristically anxious, "but something urgent has come up."

"I am listening," I said as my heart began to lash against my ribs. The terrifying thought passed over me that Intisar had somehow learnt about my carelessness.

"It appears that Riju has taken an interest in Noor's vanishing."

While I felt relieved that she was still in the dark regarding the absence of Noor, this new piece of information took a while to register.

"How did he get involved in this?" I asked, surprised.

"He is in Mumbai, *janab*. He has already-"

"No," I stopped her, "start from the beginning."

"Alright," she said. "Riju was visiting Basirhat when the riots broke out. Then... You know how delusional these people, who have been bitten by the bug of patriotism, can be. They think they carry the weight of the whole country on their shoulders."

"But he is between assignments." I was still confused. "He is supposed to keep a low profile and stay silent."

"We can't waste time discussing his reasons. As I was saying, he has already reached Mumbai. He even visited the Elephanta caves and discovered- Did you take Noor over there?"

"Yes, I did." I regretted taking the risk. "It was necessary to make her accept Shiva as her friend for the first video."

"It was necessary?"

"Yes."

She released a breath. "You should have asked me if it was safe to give her a Mumbai tour."

I did not miss the reproach in her voice. I almost blurted out that I was not supposed to take her permission before every step.

"I thought it would be harmless," I said.

"It was a blunder. Riju found out that Noor went there a few days ago."

"But we didn't talk to anybody." I was still shocked at how close Riju's fingers had come to my neck. How did he know about our trip?

"Stop speaking like a child," she raised her voice, now clearly irritated. "There's more. He thinks he knows how Noor was kidnapped. Although my source did not elaborate on it. So I am not sure how he knows."

"Un-huh," I managed. I could see my carefully laid out plans on the verge of falling apart.

"Looks like he is excellent at following clues," she released a sigh. "*Janab*, I have a bad feeling about this."

"What do you suggest me to do?"

"He must stay away from all this," she said. "Perhaps... maybe you should think about getting him killed."

"Let me think about it."

"What's there to think?" she snapped. "Just get it done. You carried out your wishes, and look what it brought about."

"Intisarji," I said calmly, "there are fates worse than death that can fall upon a secret agent. Trust me, I had been a civil servant. I understand."

"Well, at present, you are serving me. And from now on, I want to know your every plan."

I was about to remind her about the symbiotic nature of our relationship but bit back on it.

"Fine," I said, resisting my voice from getting infected by anger. "More than dying, a spy fears his cover being blown away. Because it puts not only his family but also his whole organization, in danger."

"How do you know that the RAW did not assign him for this in the first place?"

"I can easily find that out from his boss," I assured her. "And if Venkat has no idea about what Riju is up to, I would be happy to inform him."

There was no sound from the other side for a minute.

"Okay," she said finally. "Talk to Venkat. However, you must be careful of something else."

"Yes?"

"My daughter is also with Riju. Don't cause her any harm. Initially, I thought I would ask her to stay away from him. But then I decided she could keep us informed on Riju's activities."

"Does she know-?"

"She knows nothing about us. And it must remain that way."

"I understand," I said, "she will be safe. But how did she end up with Riju?"

"She wants to rescue Noor."

"Congratulations. You have raised a daughter who cares for the country." I meant it as a snide remark. Behind the veil of nationalism, Intisar only cared for power.

"Aziza's love for the nation is not very different from ours," she said, missing my sarcasm. "Except she does not understand yet that sometimes, for protecting our loved ones, we need to drink poison."

Our conversation ended. Intisar's last words were valid, at least for me. I was the Neel-Kanth of the society. This country was my beloved; I killed a small decayed portion of its body every day so that she stayed healthy. And along the way, I died a little bit inside every day. But I considered it a small payment.

I tried to remember what clues I had left behind. Riju's progress surprised and scared me. There were other agents in the RAW with more diverse skills than him. On a couple of occasions, I had heard that he had broken the protocols to achieve his objective. His track record was not impeccable in how he worked but perfect for successful results. It was why Venkat had chosen Riju for the mission in South Africa.

I remembered Venkat once saying, "Riju is not reckless, but unorthodox. When he is deployed for an assignment, many people in the agency secretly hold their breaths. I am one of them." But Noor's disappearance was not an official mission. I wondered how Venkat would react if he knew about Riju's ongoing irresponsible adventures.

Chapter 19

Riju

I reached Dhritiman on his mobile three times since morning. Every time I learnt that there had been no progress in identifying the kidnapper. Thus dejected, Aziza and I sat in the rooftop restaurant of the hotel, plates of half-finished sandwiches lying on the table between us.

She peered out through the wide glass window at a building that rose so high that one might think it was sketched on the surface of the sky. I knew that my cup of coffee was growing cold but did not feel like touching it. Aziza's phone, which was kept face down on the table, vibrated once, then stopped. A subject that had been worrying me for some time, I decided to clarify now.

"Before," I said to her, "in your room, when I was waiting for you to finish your shower, your phone rang twice."

She turned her face, but instead of looking at me, she picked up her sandwich and bit into it.

"Is anything bothering you?" I asked her.

"No," she said.

"Are you sure?"

"Yes," she paused, sipping the remaining juice from her glass. "Did you see- back in my room, did you see who was calling me?"

"It was your mother," I said. "I hope she knows that you are here."

"I told her this morning. I can't lie to her."

"Did you tell her everything?"

"Not everything, but I gave her a fair idea of what we have been doing."

"Was it necessary to tell her that?" I said as a feeling of being betrayed spread across my chest.

Aziza did not reply at once. She watched the faraway traffic, which pushed forth laboriously, as though against an invisible force. Every now and then, a vehicle would find the relief of an empty stretch and rush to fill it up.

"Aziza, you should not have told her. I am concerned about my name getting involved in all this. You knew that."

"I was asking for help," she looked at me. "She has many connections in Mumbai. I thought she could help."

"You should have consulted with me before speaking to her."

"I wanted to tell you about it. I- it is something you won't understand."

"Let me know first, then see if I understand."

She stuffed the last bite of the sandwich into her mouth. She rubbed her hands together over the plate to get rid of the crumbs.

"Everything I have done in my life," she said, "I have done in the shadow of my mother. She is so formidable, with such amazing ability to move the masses, I am afraid I will never be half good a leader as she is."

"So that puts you under constant pressure?"

"No, not really. I am proud of her. For all the things she has done for everyone, I love her deeply. But it also makes me want to help her achieve greater heights."

"In what ways?"

"She dreams of becoming the Prime Minister one day, and she deserves it. No one else is more deserving than her. But do you understand how much it takes to become a Muslim woman Prime Minister of India? All eyes on you, millions of fingers pointed at you, waiting for your failure. She cannot put even a single step wrong, either in personal life or public life."

I waited for her to continue, stopping myself from pointing out her mistake.

"I will do everything in my capacity to support her," she said.

"Earlier, you said you wanted her help. But now you are suggesting that you want to help her."

"It is true both ways," she said. "I came here. I got myself involved in Noor's disappearance because I care for her. I care for every child in this country. But I also..." she paused before adding, "I joined you so that I could find Noor and show it as another success for my mother. She would tell the world that our party Insaaf Dal played a big role in resolving the riot."

"And the Prime Minister? What about the police force that is constantly working to catch the perpetrator?"

"Please don't misunderstand me," she pleaded. "I am not saying anything against the present government. In fact, I think Suryajit Prasad is a great man, which makes our task of defeating him in the elections even more difficult."

"And which makes your success in rescuing Noor even more important. Politics, that's what you drag everything down to."

"At least it's not dirty politics. It's in the best interest of..." Aziza paused, letting the rest of the sentence go unsaid. All of a sudden, her eyes softened. "I am sorry. You deserved to know that I told mother about our actions."

"I was doubtful about your intentions before," I said, unable to hide the disappointment in my voice any longer. "You have rushed to Mumbai in search of a dangerous criminal. I should have guessed what you had in mind. After all, you are a politician."

She stood up. Her cheeks were flushed, and her fingers quivered as she pushed her chair back. She looked terribly hurt.

"How could you say that?" she muttered. "It's true that I was thinking of adding one more achievement to the list for *ammijaan*. But above all, I came here for Noor. For that little girl who is out there somewhere praying for someone to come and save her."

"You don't understand how much I am risking by just being here," I snapped.

"I said I am sorry. Be rest assured, I won't tell mother anything else."

She scooped up her phone, and on her way out, her dupatta accidentally upset the glass. It rolled till the edge of the table and stopped. I sat there, breathing heavily, cursing myself for bringing Aziza with me. She might not have realized the delicateness of my situation, but I could not believe that she kept secrets from me. God knew what else she was hiding.

Chapter 20

Vikram

Shiva waited impatiently as I finished the phone call with Venkat. Satisfied with how the conversation went, I kept the mobile down and observed my faithful secretary. Under a threadbare cover of hair, his scalp seemed pinker than usual. His face, double-chinned and bulging from fat, looked so awful that I considered asking him to sit down beside me. But I had realized long back that the world remained sane only when everyone respected the status quo. So I dismissed the thought of allowing Shiva any comfort.

"Sympathy and empathy," a senior bureaucrat had once told me, "are bigger hoaxes than homoeopathy. All of them work on the placebo effect. You pretend that they cure people even when you know that they achieve nothing."

"Did you find Noor?" I asked Shiva.

He brushed away drops of sweat from his eyebrows. "No, Sir. My men are looking for her everywhere in the city."

"I think I told you to not return until you have located her."

"I remember it," he rubbed his hands together as though deciding on an appropriate starting point. "But- uh- something nasty is about to happen if my sources are correct."

"Why, what's wrong?"

He opened his mouth to speak, then closed it again. He took out his phone and started a video call application. "It's better if you see for yourself. Intisar madam has called for an urgent press conference, which is about to start."

"And your sources know from beforehand what she is going to speak about?"

Without replying, he gave me the phone. I saw familiar members of Insaaf Dal on the screen occupying a table. On it stood numerous microphones. There was an air of seriousness about the whole setup.

"One of my men is sitting in the front row," Shiva explained. "He is recording the video."

Flashes of cameras went off as Intisar walked across the stage and, after greeting the others, took her place in the middle chair. She sat straight, not leaning towards the microphone, and looked at her audience. Her hair, perfectly straightened, swept across her shoulders.

"Thank you for coming on such short notice," she began, "I am sorry, but the alarming nature of the matter forced me to call you right away. What I am about to say, I am sure, will help you understand the hurry in which I have organized this meeting. Now, I will be blunt. The Prime Minister of India is hiding a lot from the common people.

He has lied. He has betrayed the trust of not only Indian citizens but also the people outside." She paused to appraise the effect of her words on the reporters. "He has shown a terrible level of dishonesty."

Her figure, otherwise effortlessly fluidic, became alert. Her shoulders squared from the pride of betraying the betrayer. Right then, I realized that she was turning into a harbinger of disaster. She was giving up confidential information about the nation. An oily uneasiness grew in my guts.

"All of you know that an Indian representative joined the team which was supposed to recover some ancient scripts from South Africa," she went on. "You must also remember that these scripts might have thrown light on the birth of a religion that was completely unknown until now. The experts call it The Mother Religion. They consider it the missing piece that connects the birth of multiple religions we follow today. Imagine what such a discovery could do. It could tell us that our religions are not competitors, but distant relatives. It could provide a massive help in bringing peace to communally disturbed areas." She passed a wordless glance around the room. "Do you know what our Prime Minister did to compromise the mission? He formed a secret committee along with Vikram Rathore."

The mention of my name made Shiva mutter a cuss word under his breath. I felt the discomfort in my stomach burst into anger.

"Suryajitji also invited me to be a part of the committee," Intisar continued. "I agreed because I wanted to expose his dirty plans. And now I know he is a shameless, vile man. I can't tell you anything more because the police will arrest me for revealing too much about a secret government operation.

But I want all the media persons sitting in this room to play the role of answer-seekers. Go and ask the PM, was the South African mission indeed a complete failure? While other countries sent scholars, researchers, and archaeologists, why did we choose a nobody as our representative? Please go and ask Vikram Rathore why he supported the PM in his madness to keep his intentions hidden from the world? Because of people like them, no educated person in his right mind opts for politics. They are the rotten fish that make the whole pond poisonous." She lifted a finger towards the ceiling.

"If those two men have any self-respect left in them, and if they remember even a word from the many reasons they fooled themselves with while venturing into politics, they must resign immediately. They must take full responsibility for their mistakes, let go of their powers, and surrender to the police without delay. *Bhare bazaar mein ek masoom Musalmaan ladki ko agwa kia jaata hai, yeh haalat hai desh ki.* Is this the freedom Gandhiji dreamed of? I want you all to go and demand answers. Direct answers, not through show cause notices or bought-out enquiry committees, but face to face." She stopped and punched the air. "Jai Hind!"

Her speech ended. "Suryajit Prasad, *haai haai*," the other party members chorused, "Vikram Rathore, *haai haai*, Prime Minister, *haai haai*..." More voices erupted in the background. Letting the others take over, Intisar left the scene.

Even before I could recover from the shock, my chief of security came running from the main gate.

"Sir," he panted for a second before regaining the calm composure his job had taught him, "Sir, media vans have arrived in throngs. They are parking right outside. Reporters are shouting to be let inside. What are our instructions?"

My brain reeled under a chaos of emotions — confusion, bewilderment, fury, and above all, loneliness. Curiously enough, I felt alone; and naked, not from the lack of clothes but from a complete dearth of friends.

"Sir, what should we do?" the head of security asked.

"Hold your position," I responded, trying to remember where I had kept my gun. "Do not open the gate under any circumstance. If you need backup, send for more guards."

"What if," he gulped, "what if the police comes?"

"Tell everyone I am not home. Also, don't use any force to drive them away. Remember that your every move will be videotaped."

He nodded and rushed away. I turned towards Shiva, who stood as though carved out of stone.

"Now-" he mumbled, clearly more enraged than scared. He was the sort of person who thought every problem could be solved with the press of a trigger. "Now what?"

"Bring in every single gang you have connections with," I said as I struggled to push through a knot of dark emotions and make my grey cells work. "Tell them that I have enough money to feed them, their families, their mistresses and their bastards for several years. They must protect me now. And I have a task for you, only you, but first I must make a phone call."

He stepped aside while I dialled a number.

"*As-salamu Alaykum,*" Intisar greeted me from the other end of the line. "So it is true that the bell of my victory rings in the death knell of others."

"Stop with your nonsense wisdom," my jaws moved stiffly as I could hear, not very far away in her backdrop, a storm of voices. "Why did you do it?"

"*Janab*, I do not understand what you are saying."

"Why did you do it?" I asked again.

"You should be thankful that I even picked up your call."

"How can you be so-" I stopped, suddenly realizing why she would not talk frankly. She knew that there was every possibility of our conversation being recorded and used against her. "You are aware that I have enough dirt against you to ruin you."

She laughed a burst of deceptively sweet laughter. "You forget something. Although everyone complains about uncontrollable inflation in the economy, thankfully, *sarkari suvidhaaein abhi bhi sasti hai.*"

She was talking about corrupt government officials who could be cheaply bought.

"Besides," she added, "more people will become my friends once they realize that I will hold power in the future."

"You are such a bloody-"

"*Apne alfaazon ko kaabu mein rakhiye,*" she cut in, hissing. "But I guess it's too much to expect from someone who can't even keep little things under control."

"What are you talking about?"

"*Khuda hafiz,*" she said, "send your wife my best wishes. And never call me again." She cut the line.

I wondered what she meant by 'little things', then, abruptly, it became clear. Noor. Intisar was talking about the little girl. Oh God, she knew that Noor had escaped from my custody. But who told her? It must have been Kaveri. Intisar had never sent her good wishes before. Or maybe the cunning politician was misguiding me. Perhaps the Commissioner or one of Shiva's men had broken the secret to her. My ignorance of the informer's identity made me hate everyone who could possibly do it.

Shiva cleared his throat. "Boss, what task do you have for me?"

I felt the fingers of desperation close in around my neck. I ran the thought in my head before giving it shape through words.

"You must stop Intisar from opening her mouth again," I told Shiva. "Remember, I want you to go solo on this. And ensure that her last word is the name of the person who informed her about Noor's escape."

He nodded and went away. I stayed back, looked around as if searching for answers in the whirls of rose petals or in the flutters of tiny creatures with wings. Suryajit's personal number blinked on my phone. I ignored it. Weighed down by worries, I trudged into my study room, bolted the door, and once more tried to recall where I had kept my licensed weapon.

I found it in my drawer, between Leo Tolstoy and Virginia Wolf. It was a Glock – handy for an old man and to the point. I examined it and realized I had forgotten the last time I had fired it. Perhaps it had been in Srinagar. "If the Chief Minister of every state was a Muslim," a horseman had remarked, "this country would have been far more developed than it is today." Or maybe it had been two days later when a reporter had caught me drunkenly pissing into Jhelum. "Flow to Pakistan and quench their thirst with this," I had shouted at the river.

On that visit, the mass protest in Srinagar had been, unfortunately, short-lived. The Indian Army and the J&K police had cooled down the situation before it had become more violent. I failed to understand how the law-keepers could care for the same people who pelted stones at them.

I stopped my mind from wandering, returned my focus onto the present. Dark clouds clogged the surroundings. At least Intisar did not go as far as accusing me of kidnapping Noor. But that could change very soon. Hopefully, Shiva will do his job in time. Now for all the damages that had been inflicted to my reputation, diverting everyone's attention was necessary. If I could get my hands on Noor, her story would keep the media engaged. The need for finding the girl grew hotter than ever before.

Chapter 21

Riju

I felt betrayed by Aziza's secret talk with her mother. Deciding against having lunch with her, I called room service. I mulled over asking Aziza where she would have her food but then concluded that it was better if we allowed each other a little space for the time being. As I was rinsing my mouth, my phone rang. It was Dhritiman. Simultaneously, excitement and anxiety consumed me.

"You were right," he began in a thrilled tone, the words jumping over one another. "About your theory, *yaar*, you were bang on."

"Did you make any progress?"

"We found the kidnapper." The nasal swoosh of an aeroplane sounded in the background as he raised his voice over it.

Finally, I thought with utter relief, some good news.

"Even though it took us quite a while cleaning his face on the computer," he continued. "I swear to Maa Bhavani, his make-up looked so realistic. A bit too subtle, in fact, compared to the cheap, bright paints ordinary beggars wear."

"You must have run his real face through our criminal database," I said. "Any match?"

"We did not need to do all that," he replied. "Hold on a second..." I heard the thud of perhaps a piece of luggage being dropped before he spoke again. "Where was I? Yes, yes, I could identify him because I had seen him on TV a few times."

"Tell me his name," I said, unable to suppress my excitement any longer.

"Shivshankar Naik," he said. "He was an MLA from Madhya Pradesh. Nine years ago, he was accused of running a money-laundering scam, but he got acquitted. His party refused to provide him with a ticket for the next election. That's when Vikram Rathore – you know him, right?"

"Of course I do."

"Vikram took Shivshankar under his wing, turned him into his right-hand man. There are numerous allegations against Shivshankar. Murder, extortion, arson, damage of public property. You name it; he's done it. But nothing has been proven in the court."

"Did Vikram help him get away with them? Anyway, it doesn't matter right now. Is he a big man?"

"Yes. Shiva is on the flabby side, but he looks strong nonetheless."

"And it is in line with what the witnesses had said?"

Dhritiman started to speak but was interrupted by the clanking of a trolley trundling past him.

"I guess so," he responded. "So those who thought that a man carried away Noor had said that he was heavyset. And those who took the person as a woman had said that she was massive."

"That's alright," I said assuredly. "Surely, if put side by side with an average man, he must look big, and while compared to a normal woman, the same fellow must seem unnaturally huge."

"It would have been amazing to work with you on this case, yaar. Now I am off to Mumbai because that's where Mr Naik lives – in the house of his master."

"Do you still wear your uniform on the flight?" I asked him jokingly. "No, don't even bother to answer that. I still remember the times when you wore it to bed at night. What irony, the same clothes that attracted girls towards you drove them away because they stank."

"I used to tell them that it's the smell of duty. But the girls were not amused." He laughed out loud, and I joined him.

"Where exactly does Shivshankar live in Mumbai?" I asked.

"Malabar Hills," he replied. "Yaar, you should see the bungalow. Vikram is not only a powerful man but is also very wealthy. I hope he does not interfere in our investigation to save the bastard. Thank God Vikram now has his own problems to deal with. I am sure you heard about it in the news."

"No," I said, confused. "I must have missed it."

"Intisar Khan blamed our Prime Minister and Vikram for stealing scripts from South Africa. Apparently, they sent a questionable person for the mission. It has started a nasty row."

I sat back down on the bed. My heartbeat quickened.

"Un-huh," I managed.

"I must board now." He paused. "The Commissioner instructed me to stay back and let the Mumbai police handle it. But I could not resist the temptation of going against my boss."

For a moment, I stayed silent. "That is one pleasure all of us should experience in life," I said at last.

I rushed out and knocked on the door of Aziza's room. The voice of an excited newsreader leaked out from the inside until it was switched off. She opened the door. She parted her lips but then, perhaps remembering our last argument, stepped aside without a word, gesturing me to enter. Her eyebrows were crooked. Her teeth ground slowly as though churning unpleasant thoughts in her mouth. She had taken off her bandage, exposing her stitches. I warned her about the risks of infection, which she brushed off with a shrug.

I told her about my conversation with Dhritiman. She said she had heard whispers of accusations against Vikram Rathore. Still, she thought they were false, given the long list of his achievements. And most of the complaints came from people who themselves stood in the shadows of questionable pasts.

"As the Governor, Vikram almost single-handedly stopped illegal mining in Assam," she added. "And his model of administration has been used in other areas with tremendous success."

"We don't know yet if he is involved," I said. "Maybe Shivshankar was in it all alone. Nonetheless, we must go to Vikram's bungalow immediately."

"And, then what? What do you have in mind?"

"I don't know," I admitted. "At least we can see the events unfold."

"You mean we can keep a watch on him until the police arrive?"

"Believe me," I said, "several eyes are already on him. Didn't I tell you about the swiftness with which Dhritiman goes about his business?"

"Two more pairs of eyes won't hurt anybody," she said. "Let's go. Did you get the address?"

"Yes," I nodded, "from Google. And bring along your medicine pouch. I can dress your wound on the way."

She rummaged in her luggage.

"I should not have snapped-," I began.

"No," she interrupted, not turning around, "I should have told you everything from the start."

"It doesn't matter what intentions you kept from me. Your efforts to rescue Noor have always been honest. That's the most important part."

"You must be thinking that politics is a dirty game."
She took out the medicines and looked at me.

I shrugged.

"I really should have been open with you," she
continued. "Now I understand how terrible it feels when
someone you trust hides things from you."

I stayed quiet, waiting for an explanation.

"My mother," she sighed, "you won't believe what she
has done today."

"I heard about it."

"Oh," she responded, then shook her head
indignantly. "It's alright if she did not want to consult me.
After all, I am still a novice in the field of politics. But I am
surprised that she did not even inform me."

"What would you have said had she asked you?"

"I would have told her that it would be a great
mistake. I mean, exposing the PM is a perilous step, one
that can backfire easily."

"I agree," I said. "There is something else that is
bothering me. Did your mother mention in the media
conference that you and I were also involved in the
mission?"

She shook her head. "When she had newly joined
politics, she used to act like this. Reckless and aggressive.
But before today, I had thought that she had moved on from
such blind hunger for power."

Our conversation was interrupted by a knock on the door, accompanied by a gruff voice. "Room service."

I opened the door and saw a familiar face. It was the driver-cum-messenger who had met me in Delhi. He invited me to the secret meeting with the Prime Minister to deliver the package I had retrieved from Kruger. His face looked squarer than before because his beard was shaved along his jawline. The shape of his new close-trimmed moustache gave the impression that a slight smile was always present on his lips. In the second that I spent deciding if I should let him inside, he walked in.

"You two are not at all difficult to locate." He pointed at the jug, indicating that he wanted to drink water. "Miss Khan is still using her old SIM card."

Aziza's face grew alarmed. She glanced towards me, then back at the visitor.

"Why shouldn't I?" she said. "I am not running away from anyone."

A smile appeared under the moustache of the visitor. Realizing that no one was offering him water, he walked across to the jug and helped himself.

"Why are you here?" I asked him.

"Your chief wants you to meet him," he drank straight from the jug, "I will be your driver for the journey."

So, I thought uneasily, Venkat suspected that my cover was about to be blown.

"Please tell him that I am in the middle of something," I said. "I will meet him once I become free."

"I am afraid he will not accept that answer. Otherwise, he would not have sent me. Besides, he knows what both of you are up to." He kept the jug down and watched me move towards the window.

A sense of profound bafflement fell over me, which I could not push away. How did the chief know that I came here for Noor?

"Where are the other policemen?" I pointed outside the window. "Down there?"

"I had told you before that I am not a policeman."

"You most certainly look like a policeman," I moved closer to the jug. A paperweight sat beside it on the same table. "Doesn't he, Aziza?"

"No, he doesn't," Aziza said. She looked at me. I gave a lazy glance at the waste bin that stood near her feet.

"We are getting late," the man said, "let's leave now."

"I don't think you work for the RAW either," I said. "You are not subtle enough."

"Your boss is waiting-"

Before he could finish, I picked up the paperweight and hurled it in his direction. Almost at the same time, Aziza kicked the trash can at him. It was one-too-many distractions for him. None of the objects hit him, but we had not intended them to. His first reaction was ducking. Before he stood back up, a gun had, out of nowhere, appeared in his hand. He tried to point it at me, but I had changed my position, slipping behind his back by then.

With a quick twist of my body, I pressed him, face down, on the floor, my palm thrusting down against the back of his neck.

"Aziza, bring the towels from the bathroom," I said as I attempted to catch his gun-bearing hand.

"You must think – uff – more sensibly than this," the man croaked. "If Venkat comes to know about – uh – oh…"

"He would also not be happy if he learns that you took out your gun at me." I pinned my elbow against him and twisted his free arm backwards. He tried to roll over but failed. Although he was strong, his technique needed more finesse. He soon realized that the more he thrashed about, the more pain he felt. He stopped flailing and panted hard and groaned.

"Stay quiet now," I told him. "If you scream, everyone in this hotel will run in. That will put all of us in trouble."

The man went silent, except grunting every now and then. I snatched away his gun, exclaiming at his carelessness of not attaching a silencer. I tied up his hands behind his back with the towels Aziza had brought. Then, she extracted his mobile and threw it under the bed on my instruction.

"Don't switch it off," I advised her. "It might warn the trackers that something has gone wrong." The man protested and warned us of the consequences, then begged us to let him.go until Aziza shut his mouth with a scarf. We wrapped him in a bedsheet, avoiding his frequent kicks. Finally, we stuffed him inside the closet and locked him up.

Aziza and I exited through the kitchen's back door, slinking past garbage drums till we reached the pavement. Hailing a kali-peeli cab, Aziza asked the driver to race towards Malabar Hills. The exposed stitch on her neck caught my eye. I realized that we had forgotten the bandages back in her room.

At the first traffic signal, the driver enquired if he should slow down. "No," Aziza and I replied together. Aziza reminded him of her initial instructions to 'drive at a mad speed'. The cabbie nodded in appreciation. Perhaps every driver secretly desired to run into a passenger who would insist on ignoring the red lights like they did in the movies. Hence, we dashed ahead with complete disregard to Mumbai traffic, which was thankfully scantier than usual this time of the day. Aziza leaned back and closed her eyes.

"I think our careers are over," she said resignedly. "I have heard many anecdotes of Venkat's capabilities. He won't spare us."

"No names, please," I said, knowing fully well that she was right. Conscious of the driver's pricked ears, I decided to lower my voice. "We must focus," I muttered. "From now on, we don't trust anyone wearing a uniform. Also, we don't trust anyone in plain clothes. Got it?"

"Then whom do we trust?"

I let her figure out the answer on her own. For me, the repercussions of exposure were more than she could even imagine. Juries would be appointed to decide my fate. Venkat might kick me out of the organization. He might put me in indefinite custody or, at best, banish me to a back-office job that involved more paperwork than anybody could handle. My heart was wrecked with thoughts of all the missions he would re-strategize because of me. Some operators would be ordered to lie low until things become normal again. I would have to explain myself in front of my family members. The Prime Minister would have to explain himself in front of the world.

If I was ousted from my job, I had no idea how to return to everyday social life. Although I loved the companies of others, I was used to loneliness. The sheer picture of spending every single day mingling with relatives, missing my own self, made sweat trickle down my neck.

Was all this worth it? All this for trying to rescue a stranger, a little girl? Perhaps it wasn't. Even if I succeeded, the price would be several times higher than the return. I should have stayed away from this. Disappointment condensed in the bottom of my guts.

We passed by the topiaries of the Hanging Gardens. Elephants and horses stood as though they had drowned into saintly meditation ages ago while creepers covered their bodies. I, too, had been careless enough to let creepers of emotions grow over my good senses. I stopped myself, with great effort, from turning back and leaving.

Vikram's bungalow was not too far away. We got down from the cab and noticed that the area before the main gate was crawling with reporters. Some wore suits while the others were in ethnic clothes. They jostled with each other for space and, at the same time, kept their faces still as they looked into the cameras. They spoke with habitually aggressive nods, pointing fingers towards the bungalow. The hunger for answers made them look angry. Or maybe they wanted to mirror the emotions of the general public.

We sat down at the bus stop across the road. Surrounded by news vans, we observed the happenings.

A clot of journalists shoved in their microphones through the iron grill and tried to coax the security guards into talking. But the guards remained tight-lipped. They made no attempt to keep a cautious distance from the reporters. Ignoring the cameras, they hit every hand through the gate with bamboo sticks. It infuriated the reporters, and a fight ensued between microphones and lathis. Two reporters even tried climbing up the entrance until a pugnacious-looking guard appeared. The tips of his moustache reached his ears.

"Stop it!" His shout pierced the sky. The whole flock of reporters retreated a couple of steps. "Stop it right now!" He screamed again.

The fight broke off. Someone near us muttered that the person was the head of Vikram's security.

Before the reporters could re-group, a police van broke into the scene. Around twenty khakis poured out from the back of the vehicle. They began shoving the fuming reporters away from the gate. Brandishing their sticks, threatening to drag the reporters into their van, they succeeded in controlling the situation. A few policemen got busy erecting a barricade.

However, the fight was far from over. Aziza drew my attention towards a group of men down the road. The group was quickly increasing in size. It would not be long before it assumed the proportion of a mob. Then it would erupt. A nasty clash would start between the law-keepers and the justice-seekers, neither side realizing that it should play both roles at times like this.

The next hour would see a bloodbath, lathi charges, accusations, counter-accusations, lies and truths. And down through the gaps between them, humanity would slip.

I was reminded of Basirhat. Violence had been rolling through its streets, gushing into houses, destroying relationships, destroying even the chances of future relationships and damaging lives. All for what? For a little girl.

Which meant that she was more than that. Her safety was a reassurance of goodness over vileness.

I felt my doubts clear out. I realized that the same climbers I had thought covered my good senses had actually grown roots deep into my soul. They had disturbed the emotions that pushed me every day in my missions.

The riots must be stopped. Noor was worth every single sacrifice that I might have to make. A career with the knowledge that I failed to bring her back from the jaws of danger would no longer be a career. It would turn into a spell of regret. I must rescue her, by all means.

"We have to look for a spot through which we can enter the compound," I told Aziza. "Let's walk along the fence, see if we can find a place where the barrier is low."

"What about the guards?" she asked.

"That mob is about to start its agitation." I got up on my feet. "It will keep the guards busy for some time."

We began walking. I spotted a thick bougainvillaea that flowed over the fence's spikes. It spread forth fantastic colours like prayers for freedom.

Chapter 22

Vikram

The third time a phone call came from the Prime Minister's office, I received it. The operator sounded relieved as he connected me with the Prime Minister himself.

"I hope you are aware of what Intisarji has done," Suryajit said in a voice that tried, a bit too hard, to conceal panic.

"Yes," I said.

"What should we do now?"

"Honestly," I said, "I don't know. Do you have a plan?"

"I have something on my mind, but it is not a plan. And it is quite obvious. But before we discuss it, I want your opinion."

"She did it to gain leverage in the elections," I said. "We should not have trusted her."

"You mean it was a wrong judgement?"

"Of course. Intisarji was with us when we decided to send Riju for the project. Now, what she has done... in the coming elections, your position will-"

"Rathoreji," he interrupted, "I am not worried about the elections. In fact, I am not in a state of mind where I can even complete this term. I am more concerned about the reputation of the country." All of a sudden, his voice became forlorn. "We must control the damage."

"I think we should deny her allegations by calling them baseless. You release a statement, so will I. You can put the weight of your party and political connections behind what we say. I will ask for help from bureaucratic circles. If we combine our forces, we can turn this around. Who knows, perhaps we can even make the public hate her."

There was silence on the other side.

"Suryajitji?" I said.

"So you have thought about it."

"It struck me just now. Isn't it–" I stopped as my phone beeped, signalling that I was receiving another call. It was from Mandeep, the Commissioner. I ignored it and resumed my conversation with Suryajit. "Wouldn't it be an appropriate response?"

"Yes, maybe. It is the easiest thing we could do. However, I disagree with you. I plan to accept her accusations and confess my mistakes."

I felt a jerk of surprise in the middle of my chest. I tried to keep the shock out of my voice. "But it will further ruin the reputation of our nation," I reasoned. "It will undermine everything that we have built till today."

"What we have built is a façade," he said. "And now we must get rid of it."

"Please don't say that. We had talked about the repercussions back when we had taken the decision. The whole world will accuse us of treachery. Think about foreign relations, about the financial impacts. Think again, please."

"*Maine soch liya*, Suryajitji," he sighed in a strange, sad manner. "The citizens deserve to know everything. I will tell everyone that I am solely responsible for what happened. It is the least I can do for you."

"The investigators will find out sooner or later that I was also part of the committee."

"You are right," he agreed. "I might not be able to keep you out of this completely. But I will try and take the majority of the blame on myself."

I paused, frantically searching for other logic that could deter him from exposing us.

"What about the Chinese?" I said. "They are the primary cause of all this. If you confess, they will escape unharmed."

"After my admission, I will give a full explanation of why we did it. Full explanation, right from the beginning, along with proofs."

"What if the people think it's an eyewash?" I said. "Moreover, even Venkat will not approve of this step."

"I have already communicated it to him. He said, given the circumstances, my decision is right. Oh, I need another favour from you."

"What?" I asked.

"Please deliver the package to my office. I will give it to the International Committee."

It was about time I tried with a sharper tone. "I still think you are being a little adamant, Pradhan Mantriji."

"Alright, when you reach here with the package, let's discuss it over once again. I promise I will reconsider your proposition, and in turn, you must listen to my perspective."

"Have you already scheduled a press conference?" I asked him.

"I am holding it the day after tomorrow, preferably in the afternoon. Hence you must arrive as soon as possible."

"I will come over today evening," I said and severed the line.

The Prime Minister had gone out of his mind. I pictured the disastrous chain of events to which his decision would give birth. My career would be over. The sniffing CBI, wagging their tails, would brush away the dust from one file after another containing my case history. In them, they would find incriminating pieces of evidence that had never seen the light of the day. I would either spend the rest of my life in jail or, more probably, be sentenced to capital punishment.

Suryajit would soon find out that the package was missing. He would hold me responsible for it. And Kaveri would laugh at me, puffing her chest in pride...everyone would spit on me...my head began to throb. Just then, my phone rang. It was the Commissioner again.

"Hello, hello." His quick breaths hurt my ears. "Sahib, can you hear me?"

"Yes, Mandeep."

"I was saying that," he spoke excitedly, "we have found the girl."

Immediately, almost subconsciously, my eyes went to the Glock lying on my bed.

"Are you- you sure it's Noor?" I asked. The immensity of the surprise made my voice shrill.

"A hundred per cent," he replied. "She is in Aurangabad."

"Aurangabad? How did she get there?"

"That I don't know. But how we found her is a very curious story. On the first day after reaching Aurangabad, she hid near the Kailasha temple in the Ellora caves. She spent the whole day inside a tiny chamber. No one noticed her because restoration work was going on right outside. Then she came out to steal food from a tourist. That's when the cave's guard caught her. But instead of reporting her, the bastard took her home. Now, an hour back, a police officer has seized him with Noor. The guard admitted that he would have sold her off to a friend in Nashik."

So Noor had unknowingly entered the mouth of another danger. Well, at least with me, she would end up sacrificing herself for a great cause.

"Where is she now?" I asked Mandeep.

"In the Ellora police station."

"Fine. Inform the officer in charge that I am coming to meet her. And ensure that no one knows about this."

"Don't worry about that, Sahib. Even Dhritiman is in the dark on this."

"Good. Okay, tell me, does Noor have a package with her?"

"What package?"

"I had mentioned before- never mind. It doesn't matter anymore."

As I was disconnecting, his voice came again, "Sahib, I was saying that, my payment..."

"Of course. I will take care of it."

I cut the call on his hiccupping laughter.

It was true that from the rubbles of shattered plans rose evil desperation. A few minutes ago, I could see my destruction around the corner. It was still there, monster-like, waiting for me. However, now the path that led to annihilation did not seem devoid of purpose. I did not care for the end anymore. There was only one thing left to do before it was all over.

I glanced at the Glock again and felt a strange similarity between us. My whole body was now built for only one purpose – eliminating the target – like the gun. Enough of these hide and seek and cowardly encounters. I must kill Noor in front of an audience, make a spectacle out of it. Then people would understand what they must do on a larger scale and how they should go about it.

I found it curious that the girl had reached Aurangabad without anybody suspecting her. Had she told anyone on her way that she was lost? Had she asked for help? And after reaching Aurangabad, she had ended up in a cave. Not a coincidence, given the special affection she had towards caves. I remembered her frolics back when we had visited the Elephanta caves. She had inspected their curves, caressing her palms across the rocks. Enamoured by their beauty, she had ogled at the statues – lord Shiva, Buddha and several handmaidens of Gods among others– as though expecting them to come alive and dance with her. She had eavesdropped on the guides for a long time, her ears feasting on juicy historical stories.

I now telephoned the head of my security and asked him to get my Fiat ready because we were starting for a long drive. Before leaving the room, I picked up the loaded Glock and pushed it into my pocket.

Chapter 23

Riju

Aziza and I circled the periphery of Vikram's sprawling house. Still, we could not see a space through which we could enter the campus unnoticed. The fence stood tall, topped with rusty spikes and video cameras at regular intervals. As we neared the main gate again, discussing if we should make our move in the night, we found that the inevitable had happened.

The mob had erupted. It had begun directing stones at the security guards' chamber inside. The air quacked with the sound of smashing glass. "We want answers!" they screamed. "We want justice! We want Vikram Rathore!" Loose soil from the ground swirled about agitated feet as they ran hither thither. Several hands clutched the iron grill of the gate and shook it. A burly protestor snatched a lathi from the police. He hit one of the guards, who fell on the ground, groaning.

"This way, quick." I caught Aziza's hand and pulled her behind a news van.

The police at first tried to foil the punches raining on them by guarding themselves with cane shields. But they soon realized it was not working. So they began lathi-charging. A policeman grabbed a young man's collar and started beating him with his lathi. The effect was immediate but not very efficient. Some dissenters got scared and fled, while others became more infuriated.

As though given a license to let all hell break loose, a crowd crashed against the police. The people were equipped with stones and rods, picked up from a nearby construction site. It wasn't long before the fight turned bloody. Skulls and bones and cameras were broken; the stalls along the pavement were smashed and plundered for bamboo poles.

Meanwhile, the reporters who had reached a safe distance instructed their cameramen, telling them which events to focus on. After all, selective reporting resulted in TRP spikes.

The mob almost overpowered the police. It formed a wave of pummelling, angry bodies and climbed over the khakis, throwing kicks, punches and stones rampantly. However, they had missed a crucial detail. Blinded by rage, they did not see the policemen quietly passing the gas masks. So when the first tear-gas bomb dropped in their midst, they were caught by utmost surprise. Many of them did not even know what the smoke-gurgling object was.

"Tear gas! Tear gas!" someone screamed over the shouts that enveloped the atmosphere.

Immediately the mob began to scatter. The people coughed and rubbed their eyes, covering their faces with shirts, but to no avail. The police, wearing masks, grabbed the opportunity and thrashed whoever they saw in front of them. "Jai Hind!" some men shouted misleadingly,

"Hindustan zindabad! Jai Hind!" perhaps imagining themselves being a part of the freedom struggle.

The uniformed men filled their van with scores of violent men reluctant to go in. Backups arrived in the form of two SUVs and one more police van. At last, the policemen besieged the remaining protestors. A sense of normalcy came back over the surroundings.

"Hey, what are you two doing here?" a panting policeman asked us.

"We were passing by," Aziza answered. "We saw what was happening and ran here to hide."

"All right. It is safe now. You can go that way, through that lane."

"Thank you."

We moved towards the lane but kept lingering near the pavement. The reporters argued with police to take places near the gate. They ended up telecasting from outside the barricade which the police had erected. The Rapid Action Force personnel, who had arrived a while back, took positions here and there, keeping watch.

A knot of excitement began among the reporters as the main gate slid open and a Fiat rolled out. Notwithstanding protests from the guards, the cameramen rushed to the car. Aziza squeezed my shoulder while I held my breath and squinted at the vehicle. If Vikram was leaving the shelter of his bungalow in this situation, it would be his most foolish move ever. However, it would be the best event we could hope for.

I spotted the be-whiskered head guard sitting in the driver's seat. No one else rode with him, and the car inched forward. The cameramen turned away disappointed and returned their attention to the reporters. The police looked relieved because their intervention was not needed.

The Fiat crawled slowly as though too conscious of allaying any suspicion that it carried any passenger. The policemen formed two lines for letting the car pass through. A couple of them lifted their hands in salutes directed at the person who was not even riding.

Such was the clout of Vikram Rathore; even his empty vehicle brought out salutes. Could it be that- but why would he leave his house? I felt uneasy as the thought prickled my back.

"I am going after it," I told Aziza, gesturing at the Fiat. "I want to see where it is headed."

"I will join you," she said.

"No. You stay here and keep a watch on the bungalow. We will keep talking now and then over the phone."

"How long should I wait?" Aziza asked me. "Weren't we supposed to enter the house tonight?"

"On second thought, I think sneaking in is a bad idea," I said as I watched the head of security glance behind before increasing his speed. "Surely, you can use your female charm to get inside."

"I am the most promising young politician of the country. And I am the daughter of Intisar Khan. I can very well find my way in without spending any 'female charm'."

"Yes, that's what I meant," I said. "Too bad we didn't think of it earlier."

When the car turned onto the main road, I decided it was time for a dash.

"I thought, "Aziza said, "our objective was to get in without being watched so that-"

"He is turning the corner," I interrupted her. "I must leave now."

I jogged till I reached the turnoff and found an old CC-Model taxi jittering along. I stopped it and jumped inside.

"Could you please follow that Fiat?"

I felt relieved when I saw that my target had not made it far because it had gotten stuck in a traffic jam down the road.

"*Kidhar jaane ka bhaisaab?*" My cabbie asked. "Where to?"

"Follow him."

"Meter amount plus fifty rupees," he said, not at all surprised by my instruction. "And if that car continues in the same direction, I won't go beyond Kurla."

"Alright. Be quick. And keep some distance so that the driver does not notice us."

"Jai Bappa Moriya," he mumbled and started the car.

We stopped at a traffic signal, where I got out and withdrew some cash from an ATM. By the time we reached Dadar, the Fiat had started moving quite fast, threading the traffic expertly. My cab driver, on the other hand, was less proficient. We lost sight of our target several times until the next red light popped, and we caught up with our target again.

Once we crossed Kurla, the cabbie began sulking, refusing to go any further. I coaxed him with an offer of 'meter plus one hundred' to which he agreed reluctantly.

I called up Aziza, asking if any new development had taken place on her side. She said she had caught a glimpse of the man we had locked up in our hotel room closet. I advised her to switch off her phone and take out the SIM card. She should switch it back on an hour later. We would exchange information then. Although I was sure that people at my organization had already detected her location, we could do nothing about it. I told her she should find a way inside Vikram's bungalow. At least our mysterious pursuer would think twice before confronting her inside a retired governor's home. She jokingly cursed me for not being one of those spies in the movies with cool gadgets. I switched off my mobile.

The realization that we had left Mumbai behind dawned upon me only when we caught the Thane highway. The taxi driver had gone quiet by now, hunching low and frowning; he had accepted this as a bad day.

"Where do you think they are going?" I asked him.

Before he could speak, the Fiat took a sudden turn into a dusty trail. It moved ahead for some distance before making another abrupt manoeuvre that placed it behind a banyan tree. Then, it stopped.

"Don't follow him," I told my cab driver. "Keep driving straight. See that petrol pump? Let's halt there."

I got out of the taxi at the petrol station and sauntered off the road towards the bushes. Once I found a position from which I could partially see Vikram's car, I stopped and pretended to take a piss. The Fiat stood far away. The greyness of the dusk had already spread across the sky. So my vision had turned somewhat hazy. However, I could still make out the trunk of the Fiat opening and a man climbing out from it.

From his height, I could, beyond any doubt, identify him as Vikram Rathore.

The aged man, clearly cramped up from his inconvenient journey, stretched his back. The head of his security walked away. Vikram then slipped into the driver's seat and started his car. I began walking back.

"*Bhaisaab*," the cab driver called out as I reached the petrol pump, "that Fiat is coming again. I have also finished filling up my car's tank. Should we start?"

"Not right away," I said, my heart thumping against my ribs. "In the meantime, I hope you won't mind if I use your mobile phone?"

Chapter 24

Vikram

Clumps of apartments turned into individual houses that grew sparser as I sped ahead alone, leaving the jostles of the metropolitan crowd behind. The traffic became a less interruptive flow of vehicles. More landscape, deeper greeneries, and a soothing lack of noise filled up both sides of the road.

Inside me, however, tension burned more furiously. The closer I approached Aurangabad, the more the muscles in my jaws tightened. I massaged my thighs to relieve them of the cramp developed during my long journey in the trunk. It was gravely humiliating – a man of great stature folding his limbs and spine and stuffing himself into the box of a car. I had to hide from the same people I had served – governed, more correctly – all through my life. I removed crimes from the society like ticks from a dog, replaced potholed roads with six lanes, slums with schools and apartments, and got nothing in return.

All for a damned Muslim girl. And a Hindu woman whom I had taken as a servile wife.

After a while, I could press the accelerator with more ease. The pain in my legs receded, although my spine still felt stiff. The breathlessness, on the other hand, did not go away. My fingers trembled on the steering wheel. I was driving after almost a decade.

Kaveri had requested me numerous times for a long drive. But I had considered it a futile exercise.

"I want a relationship where love feels grateful for finding two suitable souls," she had once told me – such utopian rubbish. She had tried to find affection in me, in a place which it had deserted years ago. She did not understand that the world ran not on emotions but good motives and good work.

I could have remained silent, like so many other retired men who nostalgically watched the country slip into the quicksand of liberalization and yet did nothing about it. But instead, I chose to continue working, making a difference.

After finishing with Noor and getting arrested, I might find it challenging to get even with Kaveri. But it would be no problem at all. One phone call from the prison and my wife would be killed without delay. Although I would miss looking at her beautiful, expressive face when she died.

I switched on the radio to get my mind off the rush of anger I felt for her. And also to know if Intisar – that Muslim evil – had given out any more statements. The news channel went on about the possibility of a meeting between the Prime Ministers of India and Pakistan in Kashmir. Then, it switched to breaking news.

"This just in," said the newswoman. "In a shocking incident this afternoon, Intisar Khan, the national chairperson of Insaaf Dal, was murdered in her residence. She was killed by a person who claimed to be a member of the Transgender Union of India. Mrs Khan had a meeting scheduled with Rekha, the leader of TUI, the largest transgender people's group in the country. However, the murderer said that Rekha was suffering from pneumonia. The murderer..."

...arrived at the meeting room claiming to represent her community; I completed her sentence in my mind. I kept my sight on the road, which was now brightened by street lights, and let my mind wander. I could imagine what might have happened next:

Shiva entered the room in a red sari. His earrings dangled till his shoulders and his blouse had a low cut on the back. Clinking bangles, fresh mehndi on the hands, and the kajra pinned into his hair bun made him look convincing as a transgender person. He walked with a sway of thick hips and sat on a chair across from Intisar.

He apologized for Rekha not being able to keep her appointment. He was the Vice-President of the Union, he said as the juice from his paan intensified the colour of his red lipstick. He thanked Intisar for agreeing to hear out the concerns of the transgender community. Intisar smiled, responding by saying that she was carrying out her duties as a politician. After a while, Shiva glanced at the armed bodyguards, feigning nervousness. He dropped hints about his hesitation. How could he speak about the sexual abuses a transgender person went through before so many men? Was it possible for the guards to excuse them for a few minutes?

But Intisar gently refused to make the guards go away. She assured Shiva he could speak without any reluctance before them. No one would judge Shiva, and no one would spread any rumour regarding whatever he said. She understood his position. Even after trying to convince her repeatedly, Intisar did not get rid of the security men.

Shiva took a pause, thinking of the words of his master. He must succeed in his objective. Otherwise, his master's life would be ruined beyond repair. His dark kohled eyes apprised Intisar once again. This pure-bred Muslim, this fine-boned beauty, showed the audacity to talk against the person who had provided him food in his darkest days. The mercies of his master, who had covered up his every crime, could never be repaid. In no time, he was awash with fury and fanatical loyalty.

He arrived at the final decision with a sense of pride.

Since the guards would not move out, he requested Intisar if he could sit beside her. That way, he would feel more comfortable speaking to her. Intisar agreed with a smile, saying it would also give them an opportunity of being photographed together. She pointed at the cameraman standing in a corner.

Shiva sat down next to her. He told her about the unwanted groping that a transgender person dealt with daily in buses and trains. Then, in a flash, he pulled out his hairpin. It was a long spike made of strong fibre, which metal detectors did not object to. (And even human hands became unsure while frisking a transgender person.) He buried it into her neck with surgical precision. Once, twice, thrice. The wound started bleeding even before the bodyguards realized what was happening. Once they understood, they swung their guns at him and fired. But Shiva did not stop. He kept on stabbing as long as he could.

"...the murderer was shot down by Intisar's bodyguards," the news continued. "However, by then, he had brutally stabbed Intisar several times..."

Intisar's body slumped forward, and her head banged against the table. Her eyes remained open. So much for political ambitions.

"...according to our sources," the newswoman added, "Mrs Khan was declared dead on arrival at the hospital. The police have identified the murderer as Shivshankar Naik, an ex-MLA from Madhya Pradesh. He was involved in the Unisys money laundering scam. Several ministers, including the President, have expressed grief over Intisar Khan's demise. Experts had been considering her as a frontrunner for the post of Prime Minister in the coming elections. Speculations have already begun over who would succeed her in the party. Many believe that her daughter, Aziza Khan-"

I turned off the radio.

Ever since *pitaji* passed away, I had not shed tears for anyone. Even now, my eyes did not turn moist. But Shiva had been one of the very few people who had kept my trust till the end. The news of his death brought about a strange sadness in my heart; it was not unlike how a man would feel for the loss of his dog.

Chapter 25

Riju

"In a Bumbaai local train," my taxi driver said, "people pay two times more fare to get into the first-class compartment even though it is as crowded as the second-class. You know why? Because the people behave better in it."

Once his phase of reluctance had gotten over, and he had given in to the idea that this would be a long journey, he became talkative. I put on my earphones as an excuse to escape his random observations. An old Bollywood song played on the car's FM radio:

"O manchali kahaan chali..."

I observed the Fiat that sped ahead. Our CC Model was faring well in its pursuit in this less busy road.

I wondered if the communication I had sent out forty-five minutes ago from the driver's mobile had reached Dhritiman. Faking my voice, I had told the policewoman who had attended the call that Vikram was escaping in his car. I had said that she should immediately inform Dhritiman. I hoped he must have arrived at Mumbai by now.

However, there was a problem. Although Dhritiman knew that Shivshankar kidnapped Noor, he had no reason for suspecting Vikram yet. It was true that Shivshankar was Vikram's right-hand man. But at this stage, if the police acted against Vikram, a man of sky-high status, Dhritiman would be held answerable.

I, however, grew certain that Vikram was linked with Noor's abduction. One might reason that he hid in the trunk of his car to escape the mob at his gate. But if he was genuinely innocent or too nervous about staying indoors till police protection came, he would have sought shelter in a police station. Instead, he was driving several miles away from home. Especially when his reputation was attacked on all the news channels. I hoped Dhitiman would see it the same way as I did.

One hour had passed since I had last heard from Aziza. I borrowed the driver's phone again and rang her up.

"No signal in my phone," I told the driver.

When Aziza picked up the call, I realized she was crying. Sobbing and struggling for breaths, she told me what had gone wrong. While persuading the guards at Vikram's bungalow to let her in, she said that she was the daughter of Intisar Khan. A security man, on hearing this, informed her about her mother's murder. At first, Aziza did not believe him. Once she was allowed inside, she watched the news, and her fear was confirmed. Intisar was no more. She was stabbed by none other than Shivshankar, this time disguised as a transgender person. The murderer was shot down by Intisar's bodyguards.

I tried to find some consoling words. I told Aziza that she must stay strong; her mother wanted everyone to develop mental strength.

"What's more heartbreaking," she sighed, "is that the dreams she saw for this country, she could not turn them into reality."

"Don't you see the same dreams?" I asked her softly.

"We had many differences," she said as though in a trance, "but in our hearts, both of us wanted-" she stopped.

I gave her the comfort of a pause, because I understood that I should say nothing.

"You must take the next flight-" I started.

"No," Her voice, abruptly strong, surprised me.

"No?"

"She- her body would still be kept in our Delhi house when I get back," Aziza said. "I will see her then. For now, let's finish what brought us here. Let's find Noor."

I contemplated asking if she was sure that she wanted to continue. However, her slow but steely tone made me leave the question unsaid. I could almost picture her teeth being gritted. She sniffled again and cleared her nose by inhaling sharply.

"I will ensure that two daughters," she added, "both far away from their mothers, reach their homes at the same time."

When tough times found tough people, resolve prevailed. Raised amidst luxuries, Aziza could have easily reduced the troubles of less fortunate people to mere issues on paper. But far from being an independent problem-solver, she developed deep connections with them. She took everything personally because she considered the whole country her home, not in an aggressive possessive way, but with empathetic belongingness. Not many would understand it, but I did. Hence my admiration for Aziza grew manifold.

"So now that Shivshankar is dead," she said, "how do we search for Noor?"

"There is one lead remaining," I said, "Vikram. He was hiding inside the trunk of his Fiat. I am following him right now."

"My God! This is unbelievable. You are following him where?"

"Towards Pune."

"In that case, should I start off for Pune?"

"Not now," I said. "Once Vikram stops, I will let you know. Then you can catch a flight to the nearest airport and get there fast."

"Why not now?"

"Because the moment you make a move, you will be followed by Venkat's men. Who knows, perhaps this conversation is getting recorded as well."

"But they will follow me even when I head for the airport."

"It would not matter then. On the contrary, I want them to tail you later."

"Why?" she asked, still confused.

"Because no matter what we do, we can't escape them. Also, we might need their help in rescuing Noor. We two are not enough for taking down Vikram. He is too influential."

"I wish I could disagree with you, but you're right. So, should I just wait for your next instruction?"

"Yes... No, wait, there is something you must do. Search the whole bungalow. Vikram might have left Noor locked inside a room. Even if you don't find her, you might come across something that hints at her location."

"Don't worry, I will turn this place upside down. I don't see any servant around, which is very strange but helpful. It will make my task easier."

"Aziza, I am terribly sorry for your loss," I said.

After our conversation ended, I returned the driver's phone and asked him whether he could play the news on his radio. I hoped that I would catch the aftermath of Intisar's death, but instead, the Prime Minister's voice echoed from the speakers. He was giving a speech:

"...that no amount of apologies would be enough to placate people all over the world. They are justified in feeling betrayed and indignant for what I have done. I, the leader of a great nation, have been guilty of keeping critical information from all. Not only that, but I also take the blame for this terrible step. I sent a man for mission Mother Religion to bring the ancient artefact to India. I know that the crime sounds unpardonable. And I will accept any punishment that the justice system deems fit.

However, I want to say why I did it. No matter who you are, no matter where you are, please listen carefully.

In December 2016, we received a shocking intelligence…"

His words stirred my memories. I was transported back to the doorway of a small room that almost no one knew existed. With the chief's permission, I had entered the room. Inside, the Prime Minister was sitting at a table, leaning back towards the soundproof paddings on the wall.

He shifted in his wooden chair, searching for a comfortable position unsuccessfully. He looked at me with worry and curiosity.

Venkat, the chief of the RAW, sat across from him. His wrinkled, dark-complexioned face displayed the expression for which he had earned the nickname, 'The Cucumber.' He was not just as cool as a cucumber but also as bald. His strong, sinewy built was, as always, hidden underneath oversized clothes. In 1984, even before he joined the RAW, his suggested strategies had foiled Pakistan's operation 'Ababeel'. Although Venkat was nearing retirement, it was said that he could still extract information from a brick and find patterns in stagnant water.

"This is Riju," Venkat broke the silence as I took the chair beside him, "the man we have chosen for the task. We have briefed him, but if you have anything to ask him, please go ahead."

"I don't have any questions for him," Suryajit looked at Venkat. "I trust your selection. But you know that what we are doing is not ethical."

"With due respect," Venkat said, "Mr Prime Minister, I think this is not the time for mulling over ethics. We must decide before the council finalizes the team."

"Your information…" Suryajit hesitated, kneading his hands together. "Did you cross-check it?"

"I guarantee you, our intelligence is cent per cent true. I would not have even raised the issue without verifying it myself. I can pinpoint on the map where Professor Murakami was trained by China's intel ops."

"Is it true that he's a professor?"

Venkat nodded. "He is a lot more than that."

"And is this our only option?"

"No," Venkat replied, "but it is the best route we can take now. As I explained before, we can't directly accuse China of sending a secret operator for the mission. It will have implications everywhere – foreign relations, economy, military. Everywhere."

"I am well aware of our delicate position with the Chinese," Suryajit said in a tone of lament. "Also, their attitude towards Pakistan is just so… But I still think if we have evidence against Dr Murakami, we should present it to the International council. Let them take the call."

"It won't prevent a crisis with China. If they get any inkling of our knowledge about Murakami, they will say we are trying to defame them. They will wipe out all shreds of evidence."

"It's very complicated," Suryajit admitted.

"While the mission goes on, we will continue gathering more proofs against Dr Murakami. You can use them and convince everyone later that we had no intention to fool anybody."

Suryajit nodded thoughtfully.

"Mr Prime Minister," Venkat said. "We must take a stance. I have already told Dr Singh that he will not visit South Africa. He is getting admitted to a hospital tonight. You will declare him unfit for the mission. We have already slipped in Riju's name as a backup."

"What's his undercover name?" Suryajit glanced at me.

"Dr Deven Sharma," I said.

"The moment you announce that Dr Sharma is replacing Dr Singh," Venkat said, "the council will start a background check. We will change Riju's entire history overnight. It's very risky, I know, but not impossible."

Suryajit now turned at me squarely. "So from being the topper of Criminal Psychology, you will turn into a double PhD holder in Anthropology and Religious History. If I were you, I would be really stressed."

I shrugged. I did not tell the Prime Minister that I had once pretended to be a beggar suffering from dementia in an Israeli psychiatric hospital for six months. Back then, I realized that learning new subjects was way simpler than unlearning the habits of a civilized human.

"After our training, he will become convincing enough," Venkat assured Suryajit.

Although Suryajit stayed quiet, shadows of uncertainty still lingered on his face.

"Are you willing to do this?" he asked me bluntly.

"The decision is not entirely his-" Venkat started, but the Prime Minister intervened by holding up a palm.

"I want an honest answer," Suryajit told me.

"At least on this project," I said, "I can act as a learned man for whom money is the least of worries. I had been living undercover in slums for the past one year, and I am tired of it now."

Both Suryajit and Venkat frowned at me.

"I was joking," I clarified. "Of course I will do it, Sir. Willingly."

Suryajit's lips loosened into a smile, but his eyebrows stayed crinkled. He did not find it funny, merely acknowledged it as a joke. He looked at Venkat. "Riju's profile also says that he scored the highest grades in close combat in the RAW's history. Without a doubt, you are sending your best man, hmm?"

Since the PM put so much emphasis on report cards, I did not mention that I still fell short of winning the gold medal in our batch.

"What was your grade in the improvised weaponry section?" he asked me.

"Mr Prime Minister," Venkat said, "all my operators are equally brilliant. It is always a question of who is available and best suited for the job. I prefer Riju for this because he has a very flexible base-level character. He builds his personality for the job in the same way as a method actor."

Yes, I was a method actor. Only that, instead of my career, my life depended on acting.

After signing approval documents, Suryajit seemed a little relieved as he rose from his chair. He reminded us that we were up against the same neighbour who had exposed holes in our strategies during the Sino-India war. That event had resulted in the birth of the RAW. Then Suryajit extended a hand towards me.

"It was nice meeting you," he said. "Now, let's go back to being strangers."

He went out through the buzzer-locked door. Venkat and I stayed back. Saying that we needed a plan for my preparatory period, the chief produced his notebook from his bag. He favoured a pen-paper over a laptop for initial drafts when ideas were still fuzzy. Our logo was embossed on his notebook's leather cover – the National Emblem enclosed by olive leaves shaped like wings. Underneath it sparkled the words, "*Dharmo Rakshati Rakshit*", "The law protects when it is protected."

Unlike the defence forces, we could not carry our badges on the clothes we wore. But, nonetheless, we held it in our hearts. My duty taught me that pride in one's job could give one goose-bumps.

Now, my remembrance of the small room ended. The Prime Minister's voice was still pouring out from the car's speakers.

"...repeat that I take full responsibility for our steps. Everyone else involved merely acted on my orders. I will step down at this very moment if most people feel that I am no longer suitable for my position. If any party moves a no-confidence motion against me in the Parliament, I will face it without hesitation.

The UN will soon have the artefact that we retrieved from South Africa. You can trust me. It has not been opened or tampered with in any way. And I will submit a detailed explanation and proof showing that the representative sent by our neighbouring country was a member of their intelligence agency. And unlike our representative, he had no plans of retrieving the artefact unharmed. He wanted to destroy it because his country's intelligence believed that the Mother Religion contained verses that might be blasphemous to Buddhism. They were scared that their religion would be threatened to lose followers in hordes.

Today is a black day. Today we lost one of the most outstanding leaders of the nation. The most fitting homage I can pay to the late Intisar Khan is coming clean and honest with everyone. She had always been a proponent of transparency. I hope she can hear me when I say that both of us had the best intentions when we took the decision. She lifted an enormous weight from my chest by making the secret public. Hence I respect her even more now. May she rest in peace. Jai Hind!"

Once the speech was over, my taxi driver squinted at a road sign. "It looks like the Fiat is moving towards Aurangabad," he said. "It will be meter plus three hundred rupees."

Chapter 26

Vikram

I spent the night at a luxury hotel in Aurangabad. The tremendous thrill flowing in my veins kept me awake. I had finally reached my target. I was so close to Noor that I could almost smell her rose attar, that distinct fragrance of a Muslim girl, the smell of a sacrificial goat. The feeling of pleasure I had experienced when I touched her soft flesh returned in my fingers. An incredible mixture of hatred and lust overpowered my senses.

I drove for less than two hours in the morning and turned my car into the Khuldabad Police Station parking. A constable flung the door open for me. He saluted hard enough to cause his old, feeble figure to spring up in the air. He announced that Commissioner Mandeep had informed them about my arrival. Then, he tossed a marigold garland around my neck.

"Come this way, Sir." He bowed and led me inside. The Officer in Charge, Gagan Chaturvedi, welcomed me with a grin that looked like an explosion of teeth.

"Chai and samosa, Sir?" he asked. He slapped a chair clean with his handkerchief before motioning me towards it.

"No, thank you," I said. "Please call for Noor. I would like to take her with me right now."

"Excuse me," he looked puzzled as his haphazard teeth rematerialized, "I don't understand. What do you mean, taking the girl with you?"

"Oh, I am sorry," I said, "I forgot to explain the situation. You must be aware that Noor was kidnapped from Basirhat. And it resulted in a communal riot that is still-"

"Yes," he cut in, wobbling his head, "I know, I know. That's why as soon as I realized that Noor is the missing girl from Basirhat, I called up my superior, who in turn informed Commissioner Mandeep Chawla."

"You did a great job by rescuing the girl."

He grinned again and received the compliment with folded hands.

"And the information kept climbing up and up," I continued. "Once it reached the Prime Minister's ears, he asked for my help in returning Noor to her home. So now, Dilon Main Mohabbat and the police will jointly deliver the girl to her mother."

"I understand," he said gleefully. He then summoned the frail constable and told him, "Ask Pramila to bring the girl."

"Sir, with burqa or without burqa?"

The Inspector glowered at him.

"And the package which she was carrying," I said. "Please bring that too."

The constable departed.

"You see," Gagan turned at me, "Commissioner Mandeep did not give me the full account. All he said was that you would come and meet Noor. Well, in the meantime, let me prepare the release documents." He began opening a file on his table.

"No need for them," I pressed the file close. "I will take care of everything. After a quick visit to the caves, I will leave for Basirhat. Every second of delay will bring about more killings."

Gagan wobbled his head again as though such a simple logic should have occurred to him before.

The constable returned. "Pramila is dressing up the girl," he said. "They will be here in a minute."

"Actually," I asked the constable, "could you please do me a favour?"

"Sure, Sir."

"Could you please make Noor sit inside my car? Tell her that she would be joined by someone. She might freak out when she sees another stranger carrying her away. Kidnapping must have been a great shock for her. Also, please lock the car doors."

"But then..." the constable hesitated, shuffling his feet this way and that.

"Relax," I assured him, "once I steer the car towards the Ellora caves, she will know that I am not a bad person.

She will understand that we are going on a trip. The caves are located nearby, right?"

"Only ten minutes from here, Sir." The constable said and looked at Gagan, who nodded his approval.

"Here, take the keys," I tossed the keys of my Fiat at the constable. "Don't forget to switch on the AC."

As the constable left, I thanked Gagan and asked him for the serial numbers of the most gorgeous caves. He remarked that the Kailasha temple was far more beautifully intricate than all its adjoining caves taken together. He stopped once the constable returned.

"She is in the car, Sir," the constable said with another salute that launched his feet off the floor.

"Thank you, Inspector Gagan," I stood up and shook hands with the Inspector. "And constable... sorry I missed your name?"

"Shambhunath Trivedi, Sir."

"Thank you, Shambhunath."

After appreciating the work of the policemen once again, I rushed out of the police station. This time, I resolved, I would not let Noor out of my sight. As I approached the Fiat, my heart rapped against my ribs. My breaths, stale and tired until now, suddenly quickened.

I jumped inside the car and immediately locked all the doors. A loud cry shot up from the backseat, but I paid no heed to it. I drove the Fiat out of the police station premises and sped it onto the main road. Tiny fists rained punches on my back. They did not hurt me, as though my body had grown numb to pain. Or perhaps the girl had no strength left in her muscles.

When her frail-boned arms wrapped around my neck, weakly attempting to strangulate me, I guffawed. She bit my ear, and I laughed even more. She tried to jab fingers inside my eyes, but I twisted them away. Was this, what I felt, known as delirious happiness? Was this, what I felt, known as invincibility?

Her helplessness detonated. She banged on the windows and shrieked for help. However, my soundproof, bulletproof car quietly absorbed all the violence she could inflict. It served as the perfect cage for the sparrow that frenetically crashed against its doors, again and again.

Noor knew she was doomed.

Chapter 27

Riju

I had made all the necessary arrangements last night. Observing Vikram take up a hotel, I had booked a hotel room down the same street. Then I had told Aziza that she should come down to Aurangabad in the morning. No, again, she need not worry about being followed because she could not avoid it.

Yesterday, getting a bike on rent in the late hours had been difficult. But I had persuaded the hotel manager to lend me his Honda Activa for six hundred fifty rupees an hour. He had quoted an exorbitant price, I knew, but I had no other option. I had spent the rest of the night at the window of my room, keeping a watch on Vikram's hotel.

I had forgotten when I had last slept sufficiently; whoever thought that all honest men were blessed with good night's sleep had little idea of life in the defence forces. Years ago, during the first leg of training with the Indian commandos, my in-charge had ordered me to wake up one hour earlier than the previous day. In a week, my biological clock had been broken, my sleeping cycle crunched. Since then, sleep had become a guest who kept knocking at the door but could not enter unless I gave it permission. Also, sleeplessness had never again meddled with my clear thinking.

I developed the habit of having no habit at all.

Aziza informed me early in the morning that her flight was delayed indefinitely. It struck me as a matter of anxiety. But there was no time for pondering upon it. Vikram's car left the hotel, and I followed him. I rode along roads that narrowed down as they passed through one of the fifty-two Mughal-style entrances. Aurangzeb had built these gates with stones now broken by saplings and plastered in patches. Even though I was riding under the open sky, I felt like moving from one room to another in someone's giant home.

Parking the Activa behind a tea stall outside the Khuldabad police station, I waited for Vikram. In a while, his car emerged and raced towards the main road.

I followed the white Fiat in the direction of the caves. Dust particles clinging to the vehicle stopped the sun from glazing off its surface. It resulted in a matte-white finish, except the windows, which still shone. I sped up and lingered close to it as it took another turn. Through the branches of trees, I noticed a hand thump on the window. It was visible once, then it went away. It was the palm of a child.

It was Noor.

The shock hit me so hard that my hands jerked, and the front wheel of the scooty wobbled. I thanked God for Noor being still alive. But she was caught inside the jaws of the devil.

Vikram's car stalled by the roadside in a lonely area. The flow of crowds towards the caves had not started yet. While no shops stood in the vicinity, rocky soil spread on both sides of the road.

Stopping behind him at a distance, I activated my phone. It did not matter anymore if my signal was being traced because I had a visual on Noor. I called up Aziza. Her phone was unreachable. I saw a message from her saying, *"I am taking off,"* that was sent more than two hours back. Hence she must have already reached Aurangabad. Maybe she was inside a cab now. I dropped her an SMS that said, *"Vikram has Noor. They are moving towards the Ellora caves. Come here quickly."* Then I opened up Dhritiman's contact and messaged him – *"Noor is in the Ellora caves, Aurangabad. Come fast."* I returned my attention to the Fiat.

What was Vikram doing?

As time passed, my concern was turning into fear. Was Vikram hurting Noor inside? The vehicle showed no movement. I parked my scooty. I went into the shade of a tree that stood a few metres away from Vikram's car. Positioning myself behind the tree, I tried to listen if any sound came from the vehicle. But apart from the occasional automobile whooshing past on the road, the surroundings remained silent. It seemed, for reasons I could not pinpoint, portentous. Somehow it reminded me of the quietness back in my Kruger tent when the merciless fire had attacked us.

I considered rushing to the car and tackling Vikram, then snatching away Noor from him. With this thought, just as I peeked out, the Fiat jumped into life.

I ran back to the Activa. I resumed following the car. I noticed, with growing discomfort, that Noor's hand did not slap against the window glass anymore.

Soon we reached the Ellora caves. Noticing Vikram's car approach the ticket counter that stood in one corner, I parked my two-wheeler across the road. The expanse between the main road and the caves had been beautified. Waist-high shrubs – red, yellow and green – spread forth, forming obedient patterns, carpeting the soil that looked incapable of such fertile burst of colours. It seemed delightful and odd, as though they did not belong in this rocky stretch. Paved trails zigzagged between flowers that grew in seemingly steroidal abundance.

Uniformed guards patrolled the area while a few tourists emerged from their cars. In the distance, I could see the dark caves crouching low.

Vikram came out from his car and stretched, arching his spine and straightening his arms skyward. He looked around as if trying to locate someone who could help him. This was my opportunity. I crossed the road and began to walk fast towards him, shielding myself now and then by crouching behind shrubs and taking cover behind closed shops made of bamboo. I knew that if Vikram turned around, he might spot me, but I did not worry about the risk. A few more steps would take me close enough, I thought. Then, even if he found me out, his aged muscles would react too slowly. I would have sufficient time to lunge and take him down. Since all doubts had now evaporated from my mind, I could confront him head-on.

My every muscle taut from tension, I tiptoed ahead — blood pulsed against my eardrums. I hoped Vikram could not hear it. He waved at one of the guards, attempting to attract his attention. I was now so close that I could peer inside the back window of the Fiat. Through the semi-darkness, I saw no one in the backseat. She must be tucked away somewhere.

I crouched low. I could now hear the scrabbling of Vikram's shoes against gravels as he took a few steps towards the guard, calling out to him. I considered bursting into a sprint followed by a final manoeuvre that would help me overpower Vikram on the ground. But before I could decide, his hand went to the pocket of his trousers and touched upon a bulge.

Without delay, I stepped back.

I swiftly moved away from the car and hurried towards a cluster of shops, not looking back all through the way. My thoughts went wild as I hid behind a tarpaulin that someone had left hanging from a bamboo. I took deep breaths, silently cursing myself for underestimating Vikram.

He was carrying a gun.

I must wait. I should not have thrown away the weapon I had seized from the mysterious man back in the Mumbai hotel room, I thought ruefully.

Chapter 28

Vikram

As I drove towards the caves, I wondered how to avoid everyone's eyes while carrying Noor inside the compound of the caves. That's when I remembered that I had duct tape somewhere inside my car for emergency purposes. I found it in a small compartment near the dashboard. The incessant wails from the back seat had not bothered me. Like numerous visionaries, I had grown a shell of emotional detachment.

I stopped the car in the middle of a clearing by the road. I squeezed myself over the front seat and moved onto the back seat. Noor stared at me, her face framed by the blackness of her burqa. It made her terror-stricken eyes look more prominent. As I shoved her down and straddled her, I felt her chest heaving under my crotch. It turned me on. The promise of breasts was more arousing than fully-grown breasts. Her skin had not been touched with lust before, I knew. I stopped myself from going further right then.

I wrapped a long strip of duct tape around her wrists, touching her soft, pleading hands. Then I pasted more tape on her mouth, feeling the outlines of her lips – smooth and supple. At last, I wound the tape around her ankles. For a moment, my fingers wanted to venture upwards along her legs. I almost gave in when she jabbed her knees against my guts. In return, I laughed and shoved her under the backseat.

Then I made a few phone calls. First, I informed two national dailies that I had arranged a small display for them at the Ellora caves. They must send in their local representative at once because I had found Noor, the girl missing from Basirhat. Next, I invited everyone at the nearest police station to my show. And, after telling myself that I was not doing it just to hear my wife's voice, I called Kaveri. I said that she had not escaped the fire of my revenge. Even if she saw me get arrested on TV, she must not think even for a moment that I had forgiven her. In reply, the treacherous woman, who had once loved the unlovable man, chuckled. Yes, she chuckled. How outrageous was that?

Now I could see the caves in the distance, their mouths agape, dark passages to another world. The guard approached me, his eyebrows crooked, trying to recognize me. When he said that he had seen me in the news many times, I knew persuading him would be easy. I told him that I was sent by the Ministry of Culture. I came to report on the restoration works being carried out in the Ellora caves by the Archaeological Survey of India.

Very soon, all the guards on the premises became active. On their walkie-talkies, they spread the news that everyone should cooperate with me. And all the workers and guards should assemble outside because I would not tolerate any interference in my work. They removed the chains that restricted access, clearing a way for the entry of my car. Sellers of travel booklets, peanuts and bhelpuri came out. The guards rerouted the handful of tourists to prevent them from roaming here and there. Only the Kailasha temple would remain open for them for three hours.

While we waited for everyone to comply, the guard near me, with a polite smile, asked how I would cover all the caves by myself. I answered that the rest of my team would arrive shortly. As I had expected, he did not even ask for any document. My face was one of the most significant symbols of authority in this country.

I drove across the garden and turned right. As I passed by the caves, I did not glance at them. I did not understand how the search for God could propel people into carving hills for hundreds if not thousands of years. Those fools believed that impressing God was possible by building abodes for Him, which were nothing more than decorated stone chambers. They were under the impression that their souls could find nirvana in nature by altering nature itself. Hammering and chiselling and toiling until shapes of Lord Shiva or Lord Buddha emerged from stones.

They had no idea about the process of purifying religions.

I did.

A foot trail snaked up along the side of a hill and went above the caves. I stopped my car near the mouth of the path and stepped out. From the nearby trees, a few monkeys threw curious glances my way. But apart from them, I did not notice anyone in the vicinity. Once satisfied that the place was clear, I opened the backdoor of my car.

Noor had crawled out from under the backseat, but she was too late. First, I took the package kept beside me and held onto it. Then I dragged Noor out of the vehicle and laid her down on the ground. Lines of terror cut into her eyebrows. As I took off the cap of her burqa, her hair caught the sunlight and glistened. I wondered how much more beautiful she would look once I stripped all her clothes.

She shook her head wildly, mumbling and grunting as phlegm rolled down from her nostrils. Tears streaked her cheeks. I grabbed her shoulder and sensed the tension of cringing in it. Ah, how good they felt, those young muscles underneath that soft skin.

I freed her ankles by unwinding the duct tape. I pulled her up and made her stand. She tried to run away, but I held her shoulders tightly. Anger and anticipation had increased my physical strength enormously. Despite Noor's reluctant legs and my ageing bones, I had no trouble as I hauled her along the trail.

In the middle of our journey, she suddenly sat down on the ground and refused to walk anymore. From the depth of her throat came out a gurgling wail that shook her whole body. She curled into herself, her spine bending forward, and tried to loosen her wrists but failed.

This time I said nothing. I took out the Glock and touched its muzzle against her forehead. She looked up, confused, before shuddering and crawling back on her hips. Panic found her eyes and kept them frozen on the gun.

"Stand up now," I said. "Walk with me. Otherwise, I will kill you, then go to your home and kill your *ammi*. Stand up!"

She squeezed her eyes shut. More tears trickled out. She rose on her feet, as though in a trance, and started to walk again. Her head bowed down into submission, she trudged along. When I gripped her elbow and dragged her, she did not protest.

We threaded through boulders, climbed across rocky patches, and prevented ourselves from slipping on pebbles. The tip of the hill came nearer, and the sky before us expanded with every passing minute. Leaving a short promontory behind, we turned left. My breaths began to swell, and my knees pained. Sweat dripped from my temples. But the thrill of triumph made every step I took even more determined. I felt happy seeing a little girl panting beside me while excitement dissolved away the weaknesses of my age.

Pitaji would be really proud of me.

I heard a feeble noise behind, far down below. Perhaps someone shouted. I stopped and looked back and what I saw brought a smile to my face.

The spectators had arrived. News vans had driven through the fallen barriers of chains and had gathered outside the Kailasha temple. Tiny humans were pouring out from them. More vehicles were coming. Some of them were police SUVs. While cameras were being installed on tripods, the guards positioned themselves along the foot of the hill, most probably waiting for the policemen. Their work was made more challenging by the visitors who had grown in numbers. They attempted to push through for a better view. A messy crowd, I thought, but it would do.

Someone had found a microphone and speakers, and a voice boomed through. But it was scratchy; hence I did not understand a word. However, it helped me realize that the spectators were paying attention. The sun reflected off the camera lenses, and I wondered if the upcoming Netflix documentary based on my works would include this scene.

I noticed a few policemen scrambling up the trail. They were hurrying up the hill. They wanted to chase us and catch me before I could finish with Noor.

The leader of the policemen charged forward, gesturing the others to hurry up. I wished I also had a microphone to communicate with him. But I did not need it.

I pointed the Glock skyward and fired.

Although the noise was not very loud, its sharpness sent a monkey rustle through the branches of a tree close by. It also caught the ear of the leader. I waved to him and aimed the gun at Noor's head. The policeman understood my warning. He stopped. In a short while, the whole pack of policemen dropped back. They slid back down the slope, slithering, then joined the rest of the khaki uniforms.

Noor and I were out of breath when we reached a bald spot. From here, the Kailasha temple was visible straight down below. I could not help but appreciate the dedication of the builders. They were misguided, no doubt, but passionate. They had cut the stones so delicately that I could make out the elephant heads even from up here. Sweet relief came over me; destiny had chosen the perfect stage for me.

Now standing tall above the almighty, I felt like the God of all Gods.

Putting the artefact down on the ground, I dropped the Glock into my back pocket. Then, clutching the edges of Noor's burqa near her legs, I ripped the fabric apart. As she fell down on her knees, frenziedly trying to push me away, I kept on widening the split. She attempted to roll away with broken strength, but I climbed on her, stopping her movements.

I had once read in a book that some groups of the Malawi tribe followed a strange custom. They chose one person in the village who slept with all the girls approaching sexual maturity. He was called The Hyena. By having sex with these adolescents, he apparently ensured their passage to a prosperous adulthood. Almost on all occasions, he would get infected with AIDS, but the practice never stopped. The Hyena sacrificed his life to ensure everyone's beliefs were maintained.

I took off all the duct tapes, freeing Noor's hands and mouth. While tearing the burqa away from the Muslim girl, I became confident that my sacrifice would deliver this nation into adulthood.

Chapter 29

Riju

The moment I realized that Vikram would turn right from the mouth of the Kailasha temple, I veered left. After crossing a couple of caves, I came across a small cave. I apprised its height, concluding that I could climb it. I jabbed my fingers into the gaps scattered in the carvings and lifted myself up along a wall. I regretted not paying proper attention during the rock-climbing lessons in the Darjeeling Mountaineering Club back during my training days. Slipping and struggling, I got to the boulders above the cave. Through the rocks, I caught a glance of Vikram dragging the girl. To reach the top before him, I squeezed through rocks, crawled on all four, and hunkered below low branches, moving fast all the while.

Once I reached the bare area above the Kailasha temple, I frantically searched for a place to hide. Then came the sound of the gunshot. A monkey hustled through the branches of a tree. Its noise drew my notice towards a tree whose trunk was surrounded by thorny bushes. I jumped in their middle and froze myself in a crouched position.

The bushes jabbed their thorns into my forearms as I struggled for a good view of Vikram. I stayed still, barely breathing, wishing I could even stop the sweat that trickled down my temples. My jeans were torn in many places, but I did not care. I took out my mobile to confirm if it was on silent mode and found messages from Aziza crowding its screen:

"I am here. The Ellora caves. Where are you?"

"Vikram has the girl. What should we do? Please reply."

"Oh God, he is molesting her in public! Everyone can see. The cameras are zoomed in on him. We need to act quickly."

"Riju, we need to save her now. I can't see this. What are you doing?"

I was waiting. I kept the phone away in my pocket. I was waiting for the devil, who kneeled about ten metres away from me, to get more engrossed in his crime. Soon the ecstasy of sinning would blind him, and he would carelessly let go of his defensive instincts. I watched him as he ripped Noor's burqa and flung it over the edge of the hill. As though he offered it to the Kailasha temple, with everyone looking at him in horror.

His face was angled away from me. He sat astride the girl, nailing her body to the ground, ignoring her arms which thrashed about. He now grabbed the collar of her kurti. The girl screamed, her fractured voice piercing the sky, her nails scratching at the man's elbows. One of her heels kicked away the artefact lying near her feet. It rolled about and stopped near the edge.

Vikram tore open her top, exposing a white innerwear.

Noor's loud cry pierced the hills.

Hot blood gushed in my veins. My toes trembled from the struggle of keeping myself from springing up. As if gravity had vanished from underneath my feet, and I was fighting to stay on the ground. A few more seconds, I told myself. Noor would be emotionally scarred for a long time because of how the monster had already tortured her. But the longer I restrained myself, the more chances I gave myself of saving her. I was conscious of the gun stowed away in Vikram's back pocket.

"No, no, no!" Noor shrieked, "*Ammiii!*"

Vikram thrust his head down and bit into her neck with a wolfish growl. The girl, after another shriek, was shocked into silence. She let her arms fall down on the ground. She had given up.

It was time.

I jumped up. I soared over the bushes, and soon as my feet touched the ground, I began sprinting. Launching my body forward, I ran with all the strength in my legs. The distance between Vikram and me was getting shorter at lightning speed.

However, the old man had quicker reactions than I had expected. He turned his head at me, his teeth shining. His momentary surprise on seeing me died away in a flash. Widening his grin, he rotated his hips, letting go of the girl, and faced me. Only one more metre, then I could pounce on him. Through the corner of my eyes, I caught Noor coughing.

The next moment, I lunged at Vikram.

He whipped out his gun but knew that he did not have enough space to take a shot. So instead, he swung his arm. The weapon, although small, rammed hard against the side of my head, right beside my left eye. Pain bolted into my skull, but I did not let the course of my body change mid-air. As Vikram tried to sidestep, I realized I would end up missing him. So I outstretched my left arm. The tip of my fingers succeeded in catching one of his heels.

I hit the ground face down but did not release my grip on his foot. He could not keep balance; he toppled over while I rolled forward, my elbow knocking away the artefact. It tumbled about, and, as I watched helplessly, it spun off the edge of the hill.

Oh God, what had I done?

Vikram's gun had not slipped off his hand when he had hit the ground. I stood up, thinking the old man would take time to recover. But even before he got back up on his feet, his Glock was pointed at me. Vikram was fast, I reminded myself. However, in close quarters, his speed was no match to mine. Swiftly, I turned clockwise on my front foot and, swaying away, threw a punch. My pivot jab hit him on the chin. He gave out a painful wail, staggering towards the edge, then fell over backwards as he lost control of his movements. But it was only the first stage of my combo. The back of his head had not yet touched the ground when I planted a kick on his chest.

With a loud grunt, he slid a few inches down the slope until he lay along the side of the cliff. Still not quitting, he raised his head, which was wobbling. His face was twisted by pain. He intended to lift his torso with the support of his hands. But in a spell of miscalculation, the heels of his palms missed the edge. He jerked backwards and went overboard. Fortunately for him, with a desperate grab, he succeeded in holding onto the last rock. He ended up hanging from the ledge.

I knew he would lose his grip any second. His fingers were slipping. Should I let him fall? I hesitated, glancing at Noor, who was still clutching her throat, fighting for breath. No, I would let the law decide Vikram's fate. And besides, more truths remained to be uncovered. We did not know why Vikram, a man in the pinnacle of success, had turned into a monster. How deep did his roots go?

I ran to Vikram and knelt down. His face had become purple. Through exposed teeth, he spurted out blood – my punch must have cut his lips. I grasped his hand and tried to haul him up. But his long bones were heavy, and my fingers were raw from the climb a while ago. My head was pounding. Digging my toes into the ground, I pulled him again but failed to make any difference. I did not have enough strength left.

The smooth floor of rocks surrounding the Kailasha temple below waited for Vikram's skull. A few policemen had perched themselves in the gaps high up along the walls. Cameras flashed.

I was losing my hold on him.

Vikram's eyes travelled to my left and froze. I turned my head and noticed Noor standing near me. As her torn clothes fluttered and the wind caught her hair, she stared at Vikram. The Glock in her hands was aimed at him.

"No, Noor," I muttered. "Put that down."

She stayed still for a long moment; everything went silent. Time stopped ticking. Her frail fingers pressed against the trigger.

"Noor," I pleaded, struggling to move my clenched jaws, "please, no."

With a long breath breaking through her mouth, she dropped the gun. Sobbing and shaking, she fell down on her knees. Tears streamed down her cheeks. She hesitated, then pushed her trembling fingers into the other hand of Vikram. Using both hands, she began pulling, time and again bursting into more tears.

She pushed through abhorrence to save a life.

Encouraged by the addition of her strength, I gathered all the power remaining in my body and heaved. I clutched Vikram's elbow, then stuck my fingers into his armpit, lifting him up. Strings of muscles rose and fell along Noor's arms from the exertion. Our joint effort was working. Albeit slowly, it was working. My arms wrapped around Vikram's waist as I dragged him to safety.

Once on even ground, Vikram sat down, breaths wheezing out from him. His neck was bent forward, and no words came out from his mouth. What was he supposed to say? He wiped the blood from his teeth and looked upwards as if disillusionment showered down from the morning sky.

Shortly, a troop of policemen appeared. They escorted away Vikram and Noor. Aziza also arrived, and I was surprised to see Dhritiman accompanying her. He gave me a smile, touched the tip of his police cap with his hand.

"I have many questions for you, yaar," he said to me. "I will see you around." Then he got busy giving directions to his colleagues.

"The artefact..." I told Aziza.

"I know," she said.

"Did you see where it fell?"

Chapter 30

Vikram

***

With every step I took, I came closer to the abode of God: the Kailasha temple. A huge Shiva Linga was located somewhere deep within those stones, in a chamber darkened by no light but illuminated by oil lamps and prayers. However, I could not picture it. All I could imagine was the face of the girl who had caught my hand. Noor. She had held my hand, her face dampened, lips swollen from crying nonstop. The girl whom I had almost destroyed had destroyed something in me.

What was it, *pitaji*? I asked silently. He did not answer.

I observed the temple. The stone elephants with broken trunks looked back at me. The horses, whose galloping legs were amputated, joined in. And the headless serpents asked me through invisible mouths, "Who do you hate, and why? Who is your enemy: them, or your own thoughts?"

Dhritiman Banerjee, an IPS officer, explained to another police officer that Intisar's daughter Aziza had found a video camera at my Mumbai residence. The device contained the videos of Noor that were released subsequently on YouTube. The police must take it into custody as evidence, Dhritiman remarked.

Admiration always carried a proportional amount of inertia. The more profound the reverence, the more time it took to get shattered. Out of respect, the policemen did not touch me yet. They merely walked alongside, glancing at me sideways.

The trail ended. We set foot on a flat surface. The constables shoved away reporters and tourists from our way with difficulty. But despite their efforts, the situation started to become chaotic. The uniformed men were forced into forming a human barricade around me. They quickly guided me into a police van.

A constable mentioned something about wasted treasure. Following his pointed finger, I looked out through the vehicle's window.

All across the temple area were scattered numerous bits of what looked like yellowed papers. The artefact must have broken against a rock during its fall. Its secrets had rained down and had gotten scrambled. Putting the pieces together was impossible anymore. Who would collect them, I wondered. As if responding to my question, a gust of wind swooped down and blew the bits in random directions. "Nobody," it answered. Most of the papers would be damaged by moisture or dust or air or curious visitors by the time someone tries to gather them. Some pieces must also have slipped through the crevices in the stones, lost forever.

I sighed. The Mother Religion did not survive.

Noor was obviously not travelling in the same van as me. She must be too traumatized. Still, I wished she was here. I wanted to ask her why she grabbed my hand.

Chapter 31

Riju

An old woman with gaps between her front teeth pointed a shaking finger at the window of our car. She resisted the gentle pushing from the people gathered with her. A little boy waved at us, lifting his heels to peer inside, careful not to let the small tricolour held in his other hand fall. Others in the crowd were wearing humble but colourful clothes. Most of them were laughing and cheering and hopping up and down.

Noor pressed her nose against the windowpane and counted the number of people that she knew by name as our vehicle inched along. She was wearing a golden-embroidered burqa, which she had asked Aziza to buy for her. Apparently, its resemblance with her earlier burqa did not bring back any bad memories. Earlier at the hospital, the doctors said that she might need medical assistance to get over the traumatic experience. But she was a happy child. She would recover soon.

Aziza and I sat beside her in the backseat, watching the rows of people on both sides of the car grow denser and denser. A reporter ran alongside us with a microphone in his hand.

I glanced at the rear-view mirror. It reflected a portion of the police SUV following us. I could still roam freely only because the chief did not object to it. I had called him once from Aurangabad and had told him the circumstances under which I had acted this way. I had apologized. In reply, he had said that I must meet him after returning Noor to her mother.

"My home, my home!" Noor shouted, jumping up from her seat, pointing at a pucca hut with a tiled roof. "Where is *ammi*?"

Two benches were laid before the house and covered with a white sheet. A makeshift table was set, on which stood cameras, flower vases and microphones. The cameramen bent forward, eager to get Bollywood-style footage of the reunion. People laughed and clapped as they spotted our vehicle, except a woman who stood a few metres away from all the hubbub. She craned her neck as she wiped her tears with the corners of her pallu. Her fair, angular face looked sleepless and nervous.

The moment Heena Mustafa caught a glimpse of her daughter, she sank down on the ground, breaking into sobs.

"*Ammi!*" Noor cried out and began yanking the latch of the door.

"It's locked," Aziza said. "Stop the car. Noor, wait, it's locked." Aziza opened the door, and Noor flew out through it.

"Come," Aziza pulled my hand. "Let's go and meet her mother."

"I can't," I said. "The chief's orders. I must avoid cameras."

"But you…you are the person who…"

"I will sit here. You go."

Aziza gave me a hug and stepped out. Heena Mustafa stood up, her eyes sparkling from anticipation. Noor, laughing, dashed so fast that her hurrying feet kicked away her shoes. But she did not care. With a cry of happiness, she jumped into her *ammi's* outstretched arms. The mother was short, so the girl's feet almost touched the ground. As Heena Mustafa planted one kiss after another on her cheeks and lips, Noor wiped her mother's tears with the sleeve of her burqa. Their faces mushed together, arms wrapped around each other, they shook in tandem from uncontrolled bouts of sobbing and grinning.

When Aziza approached them, the mother, clutching her daughter, pulled her into a grateful embrace. Even Aziza could not escape the shower of Heena Mustafa's kisses. Aziza turned at me and showed a thumb, suggesting she was getting something precious that I missed by staying back in the car. A smile came upon my face.

Humans looked more beautiful when they turned into one delightful emotion. The sun shone upon Basirhat, and hundreds of camera flashes went off at once. Still, the three beings of untainted happiness glowed brighter than everything else.

My car's door opened, and Dhritiman came in and sat beside me. He studied the three figures locked in a never-ending hug for a while.

"Are you alright?" he pointed at the blood clot beside my left eye.

I nodded.

"Intisar and Vikram were in it together," he said, waving at Aziza. "We decrypted his phone messages. I think you would be the best person to give Aziza the news."

I looked at him, struggling for words.

"If I was in your place," he said, "I could never have done what you did. That is why you are special, yaar."

With a pat on my shoulder, he left.

***

A lot had happened since the Basirhat riots died down two months ago. Vikram's trial was still going on in the Supreme Court. The CBI had pulled out old case files of riots that had taken place in Srinagar, Gangtok, Chennai, and two cities in Gujarat, from their coffins. In every next hearing, the investigators slapped a new charge on Vikram. Eventually, the panel of judges ran out of patience. They said that the Special Investigation Team – put together recently – must collect all cases against Vikram before appealing for a date.

I was summoned to the court as a witness on three occasions, and every time I watched Vikram with more loathe than one would feel while looking at a terrorist.

Influential people like him un-united us. They tore the country's multi-coloured tapestry along with the stitches that had been joined seamlessly and miraculously over hundreds of years.

During his appearances, Vikram stayed quiet as his defence lawyer kept ranting about his unselfish services to the nation. As though absorbed in deep thoughts, he shook his head now and then, often forgetting that everyone was observing him.

He changed his lawyer twice. And he broke down in the court once, collapsing on the floor, when his wife testified against him.

An interviewer, who met Vikram in police custody, wrote that the old man was not hoping to win the case. He was looking for something else, something that he seemed to have lost on the way. He looked like he was uncertain whether to repent for what he had done. The reporter also printed a portion of his lengthy monologue from the interview:

"We know that this country has cancer." Vikram had told the reporter broodingly. "Yet we treat a part of its illness and move ahead. Nothing can stop us, we think. Democracy is unbeatable, we say. Is it really true? In 2017, I framed a question for the UPSC mains Ethics paper. I remember it word by word:

'Being the District Magistrate for a district, you must implement a free healthcare scheme. The scheme states that surgeries to treat potentially fatal Non-Communicable Diseases would be performed for free. However, this facility would be provided to only those who fulfil the following criteria:

1. The applicant's income must be below the current defined poverty line. Suppose the applicant belongs to a rural area. In that case, the rural Below Poverty Line (BPL) will apply. The urban BPL will be used if the applicant belongs to an urban area.

2. The applicant must belong to a reserved category.

3. The applicant's disease must fall under the list of NCDs that needs surgery. The surgery must not be non-critical or cosmetic in nature.

You come across an application from a man who does daily labour in your neighbourhood. You are personally well aware of his poor financial and health conditions. His case conforms to all the points above except (b). What course of action will you take?'

See what I did there? I targeted an area of discrimination – the caste system. You must understand that casteless, secular democracy is not unstoppable; it is self-destructive."

Then, as the interviewer got up, Vikram caught his elbow. "Will you please ask Noor why she gripped my hand?"

Last month Aziza was elected as the President of Insaaf Dal. In her first speech, she said that her party would not move a no-confidence motion against the Prime Minister without knowing everything about the circumstances in which he acted. She would wait for the

United Nation's verdict on the matter before deciding herself.

In the meantime, Suryajit Prasad was fighting a difficult battle. Many countries condemned him for sending a secret agent to steal an artefact and letting it get destroyed. They demanded severe punishment for him. He was more and more cornered every day. However, after getting support from the biggest opposition party back home, his speeches became less apologetic and more hopeful.

He also helped me out two weeks ago with my internal trials in the RAW. He had a long discussion with Venkat behind closed doors as I waited outside.

"My decision stands," the chief told me after coming out from the meeting. "You can't be a part of the RAW anymore for reasons you understand very well. However, given the situation, we will look at your case more leniently." While walking off, he added, "Mr Prime Minister has a proposition for you. You should be grateful to him."

The Prime Minister asked me to join the Special Protection Group responsible for his proximate security. I would spend most of my time in the control room since it was not safe to show my face in public. I had taken up the job. Suryajit had assured me that I would return to my old profile because Venkat would soon want me back.

Then a series of peace talks had been scheduled between the Prime Ministers of India and Pakistan. Many had hoped that there would be a discussion in Kashmir after ages on the Kashmir agenda. They had thought this would be a turning point in one of the most prolonged standing disputes in history.

Until a week ago, our arrangements had been on track. But then the Pakistani army violated the ceasefire agreement at the border. Suryajit called off the talks immediately, refusing to speak with the Pakistani Prime Minister. I asked him if we should stop the preparations.

"Continue your work," he answered. "On that day, I shall address the people of the valley. They must know how much I care for their welfare."

So today, I was in Srinagar, carrying out my first major assignment as a Black Cat. I paced inside a surveillance van located three kilometres away from Shankaracharya and two hundred metres away from the stage upon which stood the Prime Minister of India.

Several monitors, capturing what the human eye could see and what it could not, backed up against the van's walls. Ten specialists sat in front of the displays, pressing switches and talking on headphones.

Suryajit's speech was going on right now, in his famous style. He gave every spoken word its actual value. "...*humare desh ka hissa tha, hai, aur rahega.* And no amount of violence can create hurdles in Kashmir's way towards development. If this state lags behind in job creation, the whole country will lag behind. If Kashmir lags behind in economic progress, so will the entire nation..."

I walked up and down the length of the van, observing the screens. Even in this chilly weather, sweat broke out under the collar of my shirt. I looked at the sky-camera feed. Crystal-clear images of the Dal Lake appeared. Shikaras – brightly painted in red, blue, yellow and pink – meandered on blue water. Along the edges of the lake, Chinar trees turned colours pompously. Not very far away, layers of snow blanketed the mountains as they slept on beds of cottony fog.

Suryajit's speech went on, "…send your daughters and sons to schools. Teach them the value of education. And when the election is held here…"

Shaking away the distraction of scenic beauty from my mind, I walked towards the live satellite feed.

A few minutes later, the Prime Minister's voice boomed in the background:

"…this country is as much a guardian to us as we are to it. So let's join hands and promise ourselves: We will, through hard work, honesty and willpower, make this great land a country of happiness. Jai hind!"

All the post-speech security arrangements were made. I exited the van for a cup of *kahwa* from a stall across the road. Outside I found Aziza waiting for me. She was draped in a white pashmina with embroideries of pink roses. Her appearance reminded me of the late Intisar Khan – elegant and strong. Although I knew that she was nothing like her mother in her heart.

"You did not knock on the van's door?" I asked.

"I thought you were busy." She advanced towards me while her two bodyguards stayed back. "So," she drew a smile, "aren't you pleasantly surprised on seeing me?"

"In my job, surprises are never pleasant. Besides, I had a word with your security head yesterday morning. All the VVIPs who arrived-"

"I understand," she interrupted. "You knew I would be here." She raised an eyebrow. "But what about me coming here and meeting you?"

"I am glad to see you," I said, starting to walk. "I am really sorry, but I can't spare much time now. Let's talk over a cup of *kahwa*."

"I want a longer conversation," she fell into step beside me. "Are you free in the evening?"

I nodded, smiling. I motioned her towards the *kahwa* stall, where the aroma of freshly crushed cinnamon emanated.

THE END